LOUIS L'AMOUR
THE SACKETTS

T HEIR STORY IS the story of the American frontier, an unforgettable saga of young men and women who tamed a young land, transforming a wilderness into a nation with their dreams and their courage.

Created by master storyteller Louis L'Amour, the Sackett saga brings to life the spirit and adventures of generations of pioneers. Fiercely independent and determined to face any and all challenges, they discovered their destiny in settling a great and wild land.

Each Sackett novel is a complete, exciting historical adventure. Read as a group, they tell the thrilling epic tale of a country unlike any the world has ever known. And no one writes more powerfully about the frontier than Louis L'Amour, who has walked and ridden down the same trails as the Sackett family he has immortalized. The Sackett novels represent L'Amour at his most entertaining and are one of the widely beloved achievements of a truly legendary career.

Bantam Books by Louis L'Amour

NOVELS
Bendigo Shafter
Borden Chantry
Brionne
The Broken Gun
The Burning Hills
The Californios
Callaghen
Catlow
Chancy
The Cherokee Trail
Comstock Lode
Conagher
Crossfire Trail
Dark Canyon
Down the Long Hills
The Empty Land
Fair Blows the Wind
Fallon
The Ferguson Rifle
The First Fast Draw
Flint
Guns of the Timberlands
Hanging Woman Creek
The Haunted Mesa
Heller with a Gun
The High Graders
High Lonesome
Hondo
How the West Was Won
The Iron Marshal
The Key-Lock Man
Kid Rodelo
Kilkenny
Killoe
Kilrone
Kiowa Trail
Last of the Breed
Last Stand at Papago Wells
The Lonesome Gods
The Man Called Noon
The Man from Skibbereen
The Man from the Broken Hills
Matagorda
Milo Talon
The Mountain Valley War
North to the Rails
Over on the Dry Side
Passin' Through

The Proving Trail
The Quick and the Dead
Radigan
Reilly's Luck
The Rider of Lost Creek
Rivers West
The Shadow Riders
Shalako
Showdown at Yellow Butte
Silver Canyon
Sitka
Son of a Wanted Man
Taggart
The Tall Stranger
To Tame a Land
Tucker
Under the Sweetwater Rim
Utah Blaine
The Walking Drum
Westward the Tide
Where the Long Grass Blows

SHORT STORY COLLECTIONS
Beyond the Great Snow Mountains
Bowdrie
Bowdrie's Law
Buckskin Run
The Collected Short Stories of Louis L'Amour (vols. 1–7)
Dutchman's Flat
End of the Drive
From the Listening Hills
The Hills of Homicide
Law of the Desert Born
Long Ride Home
Lonigan
May There Be a Road
Monument Rock
Night over the Solomons
Off the Mangrove Coast
The Outlaws of Mesquite
The Rider of the Ruby Hills
Riding for the Brand
The Strong Shall Live

The Trail to Crazy Man
Valley of the Sun
War Party
West from Singapore
West of Dodge
With These Hands
Yondering

SACKETT TITLES
Sackett's Land
To the Far Blue Mountains
The Warrior's Path
Jubal Sackett
Ride the River
The Daybreakers
Sackett
Lando
Mojave Crossing
Mustang Man
The Lonely Men
Galloway
Treasure Mountain
Lonely on the Mountain
Ride the Dark Trail
The Sackett Brand
The Sky-Liners

THE HOPALONG CASSIDY NOVELS
The Riders of High Rock
The Rustlers of West Fork
The Trail to Seven Pines
Trouble Shooter

NONFICTION
Education of a Wandering Man
Frontier
THE SACKETT COMPANION: A Personal Guide to the Sackett Novels
A TRAIL OF MEMORIES: The Quotations of Louis L'Amour, compiled by Angelique L'Amour

POETRY
Smoke from This Altar

THE CHRONOLOGY OF LOUIS L'AMOUR'S SACKETT NOVELS

THE LONELY MEN
circa 1875–1879

MUSTANG MAN
circa 1875–1879

GALLOWAY
circa 1875–1879

TREASURE MOUNTAIN
circa 1875–1879

RIDE THE DARK TRAIL
circa 1875–1879

LONELY ON THE MOUNTAIN
circa 1875–1879

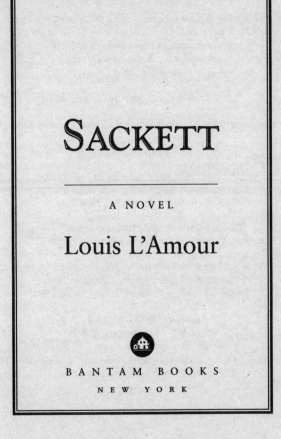

SACKETT

A NOVEL

Louis L'Amour

BANTAM BOOKS
NEW YORK

Sackett is a work of fiction. Names, characters, places, and incidents either are the product of the author's imagination or are used fictitiously. Any resemblance to actual persons, living or dead, events, or locales is entirely coincidental.

2017 Bantam Books Mass Market Edition

Copyright © 1961 by the Louis & Katherine L'Amour Trust

Published in the United States by Bantam Books, an imprint of Random House, a division of Penguin Random House LLC, New York.

BANTAM BOOKS and the HOUSE colophon are registered trademarks of Penguin Random House LLC.

Originally published in paperback in the United States by Bantam Books, an imprint of Random House, a division of Penguin Random House LLC, in 1961.

ISBN 978-0-553-27684-8
ebook ISBN 978-0-553-89970-2

Photograph of Louis L'Amour by John Hamilton—Globe Photos, Inc.
Cover art: © 2000 by Gregory Manchess
Map by Alan McKnight

Printed in the United States of America

randomhousebooks.com

84 86 88 90 89 87 85

Bantam Books mass market edition: February 2017

To Mamu

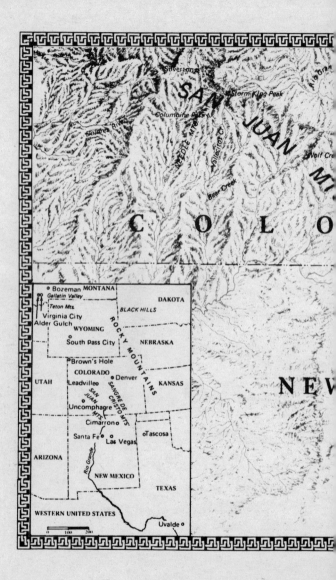

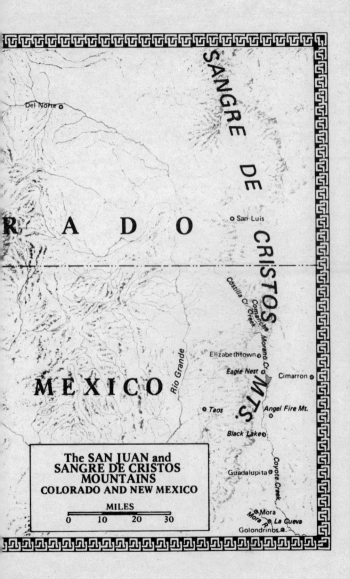

The SAN JUAN and
SANGRE DE CRISTOS
MOUNTAINS
COLORADO AND NEW MEXICO

MILES

0   10   20   30

SACKETT

CHAPTER 1

I T WASN'T AS if he hadn't been warned. He got it straight, with no beating around the mesquite.

"Mister," I said, "if you ain't any slicker with that pistol than you were with that bottom deal, you'd better not have at it."

Trouble was, he wouldn't be content with one mistake, he had to make two; so he had at it, and they buried him out west of town where men were buried who die by the gun.

And me, William Tell Sackett, who came to Uvalde a stranger and alone, I found myself a talked-about man.

We Sacketts had begun carrying rifles as soon as we stood tall enough to keep both ends off the ground. When I was shy of nine I fetched my first cougar . . . caught him getting at our pigs. At thirteen I nicked the scalp of a Higgins who was drawing a bead on Pa . . . we had us a fighting feud going with the Higginses.

Pa used to say a gun was a responsibility, not a toy, and if he ever caught any of us playing fancy with a gun he'd have our hide off with a bullwhip. None of us ever lost any hide.

A gun was to be used for hunting, or when a man had a difficulty, but only a tenderfoot fired a gun unless there was need. At hunting time Pa doled out the ca'tridges and of an evening he would check our game, and for every ca'tridge he'd given us we had to show game or a mighty good reason for missing. Pa wasn't one to waste a bullet. He had trapped the western lands with Kit Carson and Old Bill Williams, and knew the value of ammunition.

General Grant never counted ca'tridges on me, but he was a man who noticed. One time he stopped close by when I was keeping three Rebel guns out of action, picking off gunners like a 'possum picking hazelnuts, and he stood by, a-watching.

"Sackett," he said finally, "how does it happen that a boy from Tennessee is fighting for the Union?"

"Well, sir," I said, "my country is a thing to love, and I set store by being an American. My great-grandpa was one of Dearborn's riflemen at the second battle of Saratoga, and Grandpa sailed the seas with Decatur and Bainbridge.

"Grandpa was one of the boatmen who went in under the guns of the Barbary pirates to burn the *Philadelphia*. My folks built blood into the foundations of this country and I don't aim to see them torn down for no reason whatsoever."

Another Rebel was fixing to load that cannon, so I drew a bead on him, and the man who followed him in the chow line could move up one place.

"Come fighting time, General," I said, "there'll always be a Sackett ready to bear arms for his country, although we are peaceful folks, unless riled."

And that was still true, but when they buried that gambling man out west of Uvalde it marked me as a bad man.

In those days what they called a "bad man" was

one who was a bad man to have trouble with, and a lot of mighty good men were known as bad men. The name was one I hadn't hankered for, but Wes Bigelow left me no choice.

Fact of the matter was, if it hadn't been me it would have been somebody else, because Bigelow's bottom deal was nothing like so good as I'd seen on the riverboats.

Nevertheless, I had got a reputation in Uvalde, and this seemed a good time to become a wandering man. Only I was fed up with drifting ever since the war, and wanted a place to light.

Outside of town I fell in with a cow outfit. North from Texas we rode, driving a herd to Montana grass, with never a thought of anything but grief while riding the Bozeman Trail.

North of the Crazy Woman three men rode into camp hunting beef to buy. The boss was not selling but they stayed on, and when my name was mentioned one of them looked at me.

"Are you the Sackett who killed Bigelow?"

"He wasn't much good with a bottom deal."

"Nor with a gun, I guess."

"He was advised."

"Unless you're fit to handle his two brothers, you'd best not ride into Montana. They come up by steamboat and they're waiting for you."

"I wasn't planning on staying around," I said, "but if they find me before I leave, they're welcome."

"Somebody was wondering if you were kin to Tyrel Sackett, the Mora gunfighter."

"Tyrel Sackett is my brother, but this is the first I've

heard of him gunfighting. Only, if he was put to it, he could."

"He cleaned up Mora. He's talked about in the same breath with Hickok and Hardin."

"He's a hand with any kind of shooting iron. Back to home he used to outshoot me sometimes."

"Sometimes?"

"Sometimes I outshot Tyrel . . . but I was older than him, and had done more shooting."

We drove our cattle to Gallatin Valley and scattered them on Montana grass, and Nelson Storey, whose cattle they were, rode out to camp with the mail. There was a letter for me, the first one I ever got.

All through wartime I watched folks getting letters and writing them, and it was a hard thing, a-yearning to have mail and receiving none. Got so when mail call came around that I used to walk away and talk with the cook. He had lost his family to a war party of Kiowas, out Texas way.

This letter that Storey brought me from town looked mighty fine, and I turned it in my hands several times, sizing it up and wishing it could speak out. Printing I could read, but writing was all which-ways and I could make nothing of it.

Mr. Storey, he stopped by, and noticed. "Maybe I can help you," he suggested.

Shame was upon me. Here I was a grown man and couldn't read enough to get the sense out of a letter. My eyes could make sense of a Cheyenne or Comanche war trail, but reading was something I couldn't handle.

Mr. Storey, he read that letter to me. Orrin and Tyrel each had them a ranch, and Ma was living at

Mora in New Mexico. Tyrel was married to the daughter of a Don, one of those rich Spanish men, and Orrin was in politics and walking a wide path.

All I had was a wore-out saddle, four pistols, a Winchester carbine, and the clothes I stood up in. Yes, and I had me a knife, an Arkansas toothpick, good for hand-fighting or butchering meat.

"Your brothers seem to have done well," Mr. Storey said. "I would learn to read, if I were you, Tell. You're a good man, and you could go far."

So I went horse-hunting and wound up making a dicker with an Indian. He had two appaloosa horses and he dearly wanted a .36-calibre pistol I had, so we settled down to outwait each other. Every boy in Tennessee grows up horse-trading or watching horse trades, and no Red Indian was going to outswap me.

He was a long, tall Indian with a long, sad face and he had eyes like an old wore-out houn' dog, and I could only talk swap with him when I didn't look him in the eye. Something about that Indian made me want to give him everything I had. However, he had a thirst on and I had me a jug of fighting whiskey.

So I stalled and fixed grub and talked horse and talked hunting and avoided the subject. Upshot of it was, I swapped the .36 pistol, twenty ca'tridges, an old blanket, and that jug of whiskey for those two horses.

Only when I took another look at the packhorse I wasn't sure who had the better of the swap.

That letter from home stirred me to moving that way. There's folks who don't hold with womenfolks smoking, but I was honing to see Ma, to smell her old pipe a-going, and to hear the creak of that old rocker that always spelled home to me. When we boys were growing up that creak was the sound of comfort to us. It meant home, and it meant Ma, and it meant understanding . . . and time to time it meant a belt with a strap.

Somehow, Ma always contrived to put a bait of grub on the table, despite drouth that often lay upon the hills, or the poor soil of our side-hill farm. And if we came home bear-scratched or with a bullet under our skins, it was Ma who touched up the scratches or probed for the bullet.

So I lit a shuck for New Mexico, and the folks.

That's an expression common down Texas way, for when a man left his camp to walk to a neighbor's, he would dip a corn shuck into the flames to light his path, and he would do the same when he started back. Folks came to speak of anybody who was leaving for somewhere as "lighting a shuck."

Well, most of my life I'd been lighting a shuck. First, it was hungering for strange country, so I took off down the Natchez Trace for New Orleans. Another time I rode a flatboat down river to the same place.

Had me a time aboard those flatboats. Flatboat men had the name of being tough to handle. Lean and gangling like I was, they taken me for a greener, but away back of yonder in the hills boys take to fighting the way they take to coon dogs or making 'shine, so I clobbered them good.

I'm named for William Tell, whom Pa held in admiration for his arrow-shooting and his standing on principle. Speaking of standing, I stand six feet and three inches in my sock feet, when I have socks, and weigh one hundred and eighty pounds, most of it crowded into chest and shoulders, muscled arms, and big hands. Back to home I stood butt of all the funning because of my big hands and feet.

No Sackett was ever much on the brag. We want folks to leave us alone and we leave them alone, but when fighting time comes, we stand ready.

Back in the mountains, and in the army, too, I threw every man I tackled at wrestling. Pa raised us on Cornish-style wrestling and a good bit of fist work he'd learned from an Englishman prizefighter.

"Boys," Pa used to say, "avoid conflict and trouble, for enough of it fetches to a man without his asking, but if you are attacked, smite them hip and thigh."

Pa was a great man for Bible speaking, but I never could see a mite of sense in striking them hip and thigh. When I had to smite them I did it on the chin or in the belly.

It is a far piece from Montana to New Mexico astride of a horse, but I put together a skimpy outfit and headed west for Virginia City and Alder Gulch. A day or two I worked there, and then pulled out for Jackson's Hole and the Teton Mountains.

It came over me I wanted to hear Orrin singing the old songs, the songs our people brought from Wales, or the songs we had from others like us traveling from Ireland, Scotland and England. Many happy thoughts of my boyhood time were memories of singing around the fire at home. Orrin was always the leader in that, a handsome, singing man, the best liked of us all. We held no envy, being proud to call him brother.

When I started for New Mexico the last thing I was hunting was gold or trouble, and usually they come as a pair. Gold is a hard-found thing, and when a man finds it he's bound to fetch trouble a-keeping it.

Seems like a man finds gold only when he ain't hunting it. He picks up a rock to throw at something and that rock turns out to be mostly gold, or he trips over a ledge and finds himself sitting astride the Mother Lode.

This whole shooting match of a thing started because I was a curious man. There I was, dusting my tail down a south-going trail with no troubles. A time or two I cut Indian sign, but I fought shy of them.

Back in my army days I heard folks tell of what a bad time the Indians were getting, and some of them, like the Cherokee, who settled down to farming and business, did get a raw deal; but most Indians would ride a hundred miles any time to find a good fight, or a chance to steal horses or take a scalp.

When the war ended I joined up to fight the Sioux and Cheyenne in Dakota after the Little Crow massacre in Minnesota. The Sioux had moved off to the west so we chased them, and a couple of times we caught them . . . or they caught us. Down Texas way I'd had trouble with the Kiowa, Comanche, Arapahoe, and even the Apache, so I had respect for Indians.

It was a slow-riding time. Of a morning the air was brisk and chill with a hint of frost in the higher altitudes, but the days were warm and lazy, and by night the stars were brighter than a body would believe.

There's no grander thing than to ride wild country with time on your hands, so I walked my horses down the backbone of the Rockies, through the Tetons and south to South Pass and on to Brown's Hole. Following long grass slopes among the aspen groves, camping in flowered meadows beside chuckling streams, killing only when I needed grub, and listening then to the long echo of my rifle shot—believe me, I was having me a time.

Nothing warned me of trouble to come.

Thinking of Orrin's mellow Welsh voice a-singing, I came fresh to hear my own voice, so I took a swallow from my canteen and tipping my head back, I gave out with song.

It was "Brennan on the Moor," about an Irish highwayman, a song I dearly loved to hear Orrin sing.

I didn't get far. A man who plans to sing while he's riding had better reach an understanding with his horse. He should have him a good voice, or a horse with no ear for music.

When my voice lifted in song I felt that cayuse bunch his muscles, so I broke off short.

That appaloosa and me had investigated the capabilities of each other the first couple of times I got up in the saddle, and I proved to him that I could ride. That horse knew a thing or two about bucking and pitching, and I had no notion of proving myself again on a rocky mountainside.

And then we came upon the ghost of a trail.

CHAPTER 2

I T WAS A sliver of white quartz thrust into a crack in a wall of red sandstone.

Riding wild country, a man who wants to keep his hair will be wary for anything out of the ordinary. He learns to notice the bent-down grass, the broken twig, the muddied water of a stream.

Nature has a way that is simple, direct, and familiar. Animals accept nature pretty much as they find it. Although they build lairs and nests for themselves they disturb their surroundings mighty little. Only the beaver, who wants to make his home in water, and so builds his dams, will try to alter nature. If anything is disturbed the chances are a man did it.

This was lonesome country, and that quartz had not come there by accident. It had to be put there by hand.

The last settlement I'd seen was South Pass City, far away to the north, and the last human had been a greasy trapper who was mostly hair and wore-out buckskins. He and his pack asses went by me like a pay wagon passing a tramp. They simply paid me no mind.

That was two weeks ago. Since then I'd seen neither men nor the tracks of men, although I'd passed up lots of game, including one old silver-tip grizzly that was scooping honey out of a hollow tree.

That bear was minding his business so I minded mine. We Sackett boys never killed anything we didn't need to eat unless it was coming at us. A mountain man tries to live with the country instead of against it.

However, this quartz, being where it was, struck me as an interesting thing. If it was to mark a trail of some kind there was no indication of that trail on the ground, and some kinds of soil will hold trail marks for years.

Prying that sliver of quartz from its crack, I gave it study. It seemed to have been there for years and years.

I put it back where I'd found it and unlimbered my field glasses. These were war booty, taken from the body of a Rebel colonel down near Vicksburg, he being in no shape to object. Sure enough, some distance off I saw another gleam of white in the face of a rock.

Homesickness had started me south, but it was plain old-fashioned curiosity that led me to follow that white-quartz trail.

No doubt about it, I'd stumbled upon a trail the like of which I'd never seen before, and whoever conceived the idea must have been mighty knowing, for it was unlikely to be noticed. Yet it could easily be followed for, even in the almost dark, those white fragments would catch the light.

For more than an hour I followed the strange trail up the mountainside, through the trees. The pines thinned out and I rode around groves of aspen, and soon I was close to timberline in the wildest, loneliest country a man was likely to see.

Above me were gray granite shoulders of bare

rock, streaked with occasional snow. There were stunted trees, more often than not lightning-blasted and dead, and many fallen ones. The air was so fresh it was like drinking cold water to breathe it, and there was a touch of chill. It was very clear, and a body could see for miles.

Nowhere did I see a track, nor horse-droppings, nor any sign of an old campfire or of wood cutting. From time to time, where there was no place to put the quartz, a cairn of stones had been set up.

It began to look as if I'd stumbled on an old, an awfully old trail, older than any I had followed or even heard tell of.

Pa had wintered south of here on the Dolores River, one time, with a party of trappers. Many a time he had told us boys about that, and over a campfire in Texas I'd been told of Father Escalante's trip through this region, hunting a trail to the California missions from Santa Fe. But he never would have come as high as this.

Only riches of some kind would have brought men this far into the back country, unless they were hiding. Nobody needed to tell me that the trail I had taken might lead to blood and death, for when gold comes into a man's thinking, common sense goes out.

It was getting close to sundown when I fetched through a keyhole pass into a high mountain valley without growth of any kind. Bleak and lonely under the sky, it was like a granite dish, streaked here and there with snow or ice that lay in the cracks.

Timberline was a thousand feet below me, and I was close under the night-coming sky, with a shivering wind, scarcely more than a breath for strength, blowing along the valley. All I could hear was the sound of my horses' hoofs and the creak of my saddle. There was a spooky feeling to the air, and my horse walked with ears pricked to the stillness.

Off to the left lay a sheet of ghost water, a high cold lake fed by melting snow, scarcely stirred by that breath of wind. It lay flat and still, and that lake worried me, for I had heard stories of ghost water lakes in the high-up mountains.

Then there came a sound, and my horses heard it first. Riding lonesome country a man does well to give heed to his horses, for they will often see or hear things a man will miss, and these appaloosas were mountain-born and -bred, captured wild and still wild at heart, and, like me, they had a love for the lost, the wild, and the lonely.

It was a far-off sound, like rushing wind in a great forest, or like the distant sound of steam cars running on rails. It grew as we moved nearer, and I knew it for the sound of falling water.

I came to another keyhole pass, even narrower than the first, and the trail led into it. Alongside the narrow trail rushed the outflow of that ghost lake, spilling down the chute in a tumble of white water.

I could see it falling away in a series of falls, steep slides, and rapids. The pass was no more than a crack, not a canyon or ravine, just a gash in the face of the mountain wall, a gloomy place, shadowed and spattered by spray. A thread of trail skirted the rushing stream, a trail that must, much of the time, be under water.

Believe me, I took a good long look down that dark, narrow crack, filled with the roar of the water.

Yet on the wall, in a place dug out for the purpose, was a sliver of quartz, and now I had come too far to turn back.

My horses shied from that opening, liking it not at all, but I was less smart than my horses, and urged them on, starting gingerly down the slide.

That rail was narrow . . . it was almighty narrow. If it played out there would be no way of turning back. No mustang was ever taught to back up, and I'd no way of controlling the packhorse, anyway.

Once I got him started, that appaloosa was as big a fool as I was. Ears pricked, he started down, sliding on his rump in spots, it was that steep. A body couldn't hear a thing beyond the roar of the water.

Rock walls towered hundreds of feet overhead, closing in places until there was scarcely a crack above us, and it was like riding through a cave. Ferns overhung the water in places, and there was more than thirty yards in one place and twice as far in another where a thin sheet of water actually ran over the trail.

In other places, where the stream fell away into a deep chasm beside the trail, I lost all sight of the water, and could only hear it. In two or three spots, near waterfalls, the mist and spray was thick enough to soak a man and blot out everything. It was a death trap, all right, and I felt it. A man who says he has never been scared is either lying or else he's never been anyplace or done anything.

For about three miles I followed that trail. I went down it more than a thousand feet, judging by the vegetation in the valley that I found. It opened on my right, narrow at first, and then widening. The creek tumbled off and disappeared into a narrow, deep canyon shrouded by ferns and trees growing from the rock walls. But the trail turned into the valley.

At that point the valley was no more than twenty yards wide, with steep walls rising on either side. A man on foot might have climbed them; a horse couldn't have gone six feet. The last of the sunlight was tinting the canyon wall on the east, but for maybe a hundred and fifty yards I rode in deep shadows.

Then the valley broadened. It looked to be a couple of miles long, and from a quarter- to a half-mile wide. A stream ran along the bottom and emptied into that run-off stream beside which I had been riding.

The bottom was as pretty a high mountain meadow as a body would care to see, and along the stream there were clumps of aspen, some dwarf willows, and other trees whose names I couldn't call to mind. A few elk were feeding not far off and they looked up at me. It was likely there was another way into the valley, but a body wouldn't know it from their actions. When I rode nearer they moved off, but seemed in no way frightened.

The packhorse was pulling back on the lead rope, not at all sure he wanted to go into that valley. My mount was going, all right, but he hadn't decided whether he liked it or not. Me, I was feeling spooky as an eight-year-old at a graveyard picnic in the evening.

So I shucked my Winchester, expecting I've no idea what.

We walked it slow. Horse, he was stepping high, ears up and spooky as all get out, but you never saw a prettier little valley than this one, caught as now with the late shadows on it, and a shading of pink and rose along that rocky rim, high above us.

And then I saw the cave.

Actually, it was only a place hollowed out by wind and water from the face of the cliff, but it cut back maybe eight or ten feet at its deepest, and there were some trees, mostly aspen, growing in front, masking the entrance.

Getting down, I tied my horses to a tree, not risking them taking off and leaving me afoot.

No tracks . . . nobody had been around here for a long time.

Part of the opening had been walled up with stone the way cliff dwellers sometimes do, and the inside was all black with the smoke of forgotten fires. There was nothing much there but broken stone where part of the wall had fallen, and in back, at the deepest part, a polished log that had been cut off at both ends with an axe.

That big old log was polished smooth from folks a-setting on it, but at one end there were several rows of small notches. Counting them, they added up to groups of thirty and thirty-one and, figuring each notch as a day, they came out to about five months. In a place like this, that's a long time.

Sand had blown into the cave, and my toe stubbed against something on the floor at the back. Digging around it with my hand, I pulled out one of those old breastplates like the Spanish men wore. It was rusted, but it had been made of good steel, tempered to take the force of a blow.

All I knew about the Spanish men I'd heard from

Pa when he used to yarn with us about his old days as a mountain man. He told us much of Santa Fe, where he had lived for a spell, and I knew that Santa Fe was ten, eleven years old before the Pilgrims landed at Plymouth Rock.

Those Spanish men had done a sight of exploring, and much of it was only a matter of record away over in Spain. How many expeditions had gone exploring, nobody rightly knew, and this might have been the tag end of one of them.

The trail I'd been hunting as I rode south was one Pa had told me about, and of which I heard more from miners in Montana. Spanish men had used that trail for trading expeditions to the Ute country. Traders had traveled that route to the north before Father Escalante, even before Captain John Smith sighted the Virginia shore, but they left little record. Rivera had scouted through here in 1765, but he was a latecomer.

Studying around in the little time I had before it got dark, I figured that no more than three or four men had reached this valley, and two of them had never left it, because I found their graves. One of them had a stone marker, and the date of death was 1544.

Maybe I was the first to see that grave in three hundred years.

That shelter might have slept four in a pinch, certainly no more. Yet at least one man had to get out of here to leave the trail I'd found, and I had a hunch it was two men. The only puzzle was how they had come upon this valley in the first place.

On the wall, half concealed by aspen leaves, was

carved a Spanish word: *Oro*. Beside it an arrow pointed up the valley.

Oro is a word that most men recognize, even those who know no other Spanish. Serving in the army with a couple of men who spoke the Spanish tongue, I'd learned a bit of the language, and much more while in Texas.

The shadows were long now, but there was still light, and I had that word to lead me on. Stepping into the saddle, I walked my horses up the valley. Sure enough, a half-mile up I found a tunnel dug into the side of the hill, and broken rock around it.

Picking up a chunk from a pile stacked against the wall of the tunnel, I found it heavy—heavy with gold. It was real gen-u-ine high-grade, the kind a body hears tell of, but rarely sees.

Those Spanish men had found gold all right. No matter how they came to be here, they had found it, and now it was mine.

All I had to do was get it out.

CHAPTER 3

S O THERE I was, up to my ears in a strange country, with gold on my hands.

We Sacketts never had much. Mostly we wanted land that we could crop and graze, land where we could rear a family. We set store by kinfolk, and when trouble showed we usually stood against it as a family.

The Higgins feud, which had cost our family lives, had ended while I was away. Tyrel ended that feud on the day when Orrin was facing up to marriage. Long Higgins had come laying for Orrin, figuring Orrin's mind would be all upset with marrying. Long Higgins missed Orrin when his bride pushed Orrin out of the way, but she took the lead meant for a Sackett.

Trouble was, Long never figured on Tyrel, and you always had to figure on Tyrel.

He was a man who could look right along the barrel of your gun at you just like you'd look across a plate of supper. He would look right down your gun barrel and shoot you dead. Only Tyrel never hunted trouble.

We were nip and tuck with a pistol. Maybe I was a shade better with a rifle, but it was always a question.

Right now the question was one of gold. Pa, he always advised us boys to take time to contemplate. I taken it now.

First off, I had to figure what to do. The gold was here, but it had to be kept secret until I could get it laid claim to officially, and get it out.

Gold is never a simple thing. Many a man has wished he had gold, but once he has it he finds trouble. Gold causes folks to lose their right thinking and their common sense. It had been lied for and killed for, and I was in a lawless land.

Gold has weight, and when a body carries it, it is hard to hide. Gold seems almost to have an odor. Folks can smell it out even faster than gossip.

Finding the gold had been one thing, but getting it out was another. I'd no tools, and nothing in which to carry it but my saddlebags. Nearly all my money had gone to buy grub and gear for this trip south. I wanted to take enough gold out now to buy a mining outfit.

Seemed to be a sight of gold here, near as I could judge, as much as a body could want, but mostly I wanted enough for cattle and a place of my own, and enough to buy time for a little book learning.

It ain't right for a man to be ignorant, but in the hills we had school only one year out of three, and the time might not last over two, three months. When I got all squared away with a pencil I could write my name . . . Pa and Tyrel could read it, too. Only one of my officers in the army could read it, but he told me not to worry. "A man who can shoot like you can," he said, "isn't likely to have anybody question the way he signs his name."

But even if a man pays no mind to himself, he has to think of his youngsters, when and if. We Sacketts were healthy breeders, running long on tall boys.

Counting ourselves, we had forty-nine brothers and cousins. Pa had two sisters and five brothers living. Starting a feud with us didn't make any kind of sense. If we couldn't outshoot them we could outbreed them.

A man who expects to sire children doesn't want to appear the fool in front of them. We Sacketts believed young folks should respect their elders, but their elders had to deserve respect. Finding the gold could mean all the difference to me.

While I was contemplating, I was unsaddling my horses and settling down for the night. The season was well into spring and fetching up to summer. The snow was almost off the mountains although in this kind of country it never seemed to leave entirely, and there was no telling when it might snow again.

If I went out, got an outfit and came back, it would be a close thing to get out some gold and leave before snow fell. High up as I was, snow could be expected nine months out of the year. And when snow fell, that valley up above would fill up and the stream would freeze over. Anybody caught in this valley would be stuck for the winter.

Yet a heavy rain could make that narrow chute impassable for days. Allowing for rain spells and snow, there were probably not over fifty or sixty days a year when a man could get in or out of the valley. . . . Unless there was another way in.

It left me with a worried, uneasy feeling to think I was in a jug that might be stoppered at any time.

Making coffee over my fire, I studied about my situation. Those Bigelows now, the brothers of the man

I'd had to shoot . . . they might think I had run from them, and they might try to follow me.

During that ride south I'd taken no more than usual precautions with my trail, and it fretted me to think that they might follow me south, and bother Orrin and Tyrel. Our family had had enough of feuding, and I'd no right to bring trouble to their door.

That the Bigelows would follow me to this place I did not expect. From my first discovery of the strange trail, I had taken care to cover my tracks and leave nothing for anybody to find.

A wind scurried my fire, just a mite of wind, and my eyes strayed to that old breastplate against the wall. Did the ghosts of men really prowl in the night? Never a man to believe in ha'nts, I was willing to believe that if a place was to be ha'nted, this was a likely one.

Empty as this valley seemed, I had the feeling of somebody looking over my shoulder, and the horses were restless too. Come sleeping time, I brought them in off the grass where they had been picketed and kept them closer to the fire. A horse makes the best sentinel in many cases, and I had no other. However, I was a light sleeper.

At daylight I shagged it down to the stream and baited a hook for trout. They snagged onto my hook and put up a fight like they were sired by bulldogs, but I hauled them in, fried them out, and made a tasty breakfast.

Making a handle out of a stick I split the end and wedged in a rounded stone, then lashed it in place. Using that and a few blades of stone, I started to work on that ore in the end of the tunnel. By sundown I had broken my axe handle twice at the hammer end, but had knocked off about three hundred-weight of ore.

Long after nightfall I sat beside my fire and broke up that quartz. It was rotten quartz, some of which I could almost pull apart with my fingers, but I hammered it down and got some of the gold out. It was free gold, regular jewelry store stuff, and I worked until after midnight.

The crackling of my fire in the pine-scented night was a thing to pleasure me, but I walked down to the bank of the stream in the darkness and bathed in the cold water of the creek. Then I went back to the cave where I was camped and went to work on a bow.

Growing up with Cherokees like we did, all of us boys hunted with bows and arrows, even more than with guns. Ammunition was hard to come by when Pa was off in the western lands, and sometimes the only meat we had was what we killed with a bow and arrow.

My fire was burning wood that held the gathered perfume of years, and it smelled right good, and time to time the flames would strike some pitch and flare up, changing color, pretty as all get-out. Suddenly the heads of my horses came up and I was over in the deep shadows with my Winchester cocked.

Times like that a man raised to wild country doesn't think. He acts without thinking . . . or he may never get a chance to think again.

For a long time I waited, not moving a muscle, listening into the night. Firelight reflected from the flanks of my horses. It could be a bear or a lion, but from the way the horses acted I did not think so.

After a while the horses went back to eating, so I took a stick and snaked the coffeepot to me and had some coffee and chewed some jerked beef.

Awakening in the gray morning light, I heard a patter of rain on the aspen leaves, and felt a chill of fear ... if it started to rain and that chute filled up with run-off water it might be days before I could get out.

So I sacked up my gold. The horses seemed happy to have me moving around. There was about three pounds of gold, enough and over for the outfit I'd need.

When I went outside I saw that the trout I'd cleaned and hung in a tree against breakfast were gone. The string with which I'd suspended the meat had been sawed through by a dull blade ... or gnawed by teeth.

I stood looking at the ground. Under the tree there were several tracks. They were not cat tracks, they were the tracks of little human feet. They were the tracks of a child or a small woman.

My skin crawled ... nothing human could be in a place like this; yet come to think of it, I couldn't recall ever hearing of a ha'nt with a taste for trout.

We Welsh, like the Irish and the Bretons, have our stories of the Little People, all of which we love to yarn about, but we do not really believe in such things. But in America a man heard other tales. Not often, for Indians did not like to talk of them, and never spoke of them except among themselves. But I'd talked to white men who took squaws to wife, and they lived among Indians, and heard the tales.

Up in Wyoming I rode by to look at the Medicine

Wheel, a great wheel of stone with twenty-odd spokes, well over a hundred feet across. The Shoshones copied their medicine lodge from that wheel, but all they can say about who built the wheel is that it was done by "the people who had no iron."

A hundred miles away to the southwest there was a stone arrow pointing toward the wheel. It pointed a direction for someone—but who?

My gold was sacked to go, but I needed meat, and disliked to fire a gun in that valley. So I stalked a young buck and killed him with an arrow, butchered him, and carried the meat back to the cave, where I cut a fair lot of it into strips and hung them on a pole over a fire to smoke.

Then I broiled a steak of venison and ate it, decided that wasn't enough for a man my size, and broiled another.

Hours later the wind awakened me. The fire was down to red coals and I was squirming around to settle down for sleep again when my mustang blew.

Me, I came out of those blankets like an eel out of greased fingers, and was back in the shadows again with my rifle hammer eared back before you could say scat.

"All right, boy." The horses would know I was awake and they were not alone. At first there was no sound but the wind, then after a bit a stirring made by no bear or deer in the world.

My bronc snorted and my packhorse blew. I could see their legs in the faint glow of the coals, and nothing moved near them . . . but something was out there in the night.

A long slow time dragged by and the coals glowed

a duller red. Leaning back against the wall, I dozed a little, but alert for trouble if need be.

There was no other sound.

Morning was painting a sunrise on a storm-gored ridge beyond the dark sentinel pines when I got up, stretched my stiff muscles. Studying the trees across the valley and the slope above them, I failed at first to notice what was closest to home. The rest of that meat had been pulled from the tree and a good-sized hunk had been cut off.

Whoever had cut it off had made work of it with a dull blade, and to take the risk of approaching a man's camp whoever it was must have been hungry.

Hanging the meat up again, I went out and killed and dressed another buck. I hung it in a tree also, and rode away. I wanted nobody going hungry where I could lend a hand. Whoever or whatever it was would have meat as long as that buck lasted.

The trail going out was worse than coming in, but with some scrambling and slipping we reached the high basin. We rode past that lake of ghost water and headed for the lowlands once more. But once through the keyhole pass I did not follow the same trail, taking a rough, unlikely way that nobody was apt to find, unless maybe a mountain goat.

Turning in my saddle, I looked back at the peaks. "Whoever you are," I said aloud, "expect me back, for I'll be riding the high trails again, a-hunting for gold."

CHAPTER 4

WHEN I SIGHTED the ranch, I drew up on the trail and looked across the bottom. There was a rocky ridge where the Mora River cut through, and the ranch was there beside it. That light over there was home, for home is where the heart is, and my heart was wherever Ma was, and the boys.

Walking the appaloosa down the trail, I could smell the coolness rising from the willows along the Mora, and the hayfields over in the big valley called La Cueva.

A horse whinnied, and a dog started to bark, and then another dog. Yet no door opened and the light continued to burn. Chuckling, I walked my horse along and kept my eyes open. Unless I was mistaken, one of the boys or somebody would be out in the dark watching me come up, maybe keeping me covered from the darkness until my intentions were clear.

Getting down from the saddle, I walked up the steps to the porch. I didn't knock, I just opened the door and stepped in.

Tyrel was sitting at a table with an oil lamp on it, and Ma was there, and a girl who had to be Tyrel's wife.

The table was set for four, and I stood there, long and tall in the door, feeling my heart inside me so big I felt choked and awkward. My clothes were stiff and I knew I was trail-dusty and mighty mean-looking.

"Howdy, Ma. Tyrel, if you'll tell that man behind me to take his gun off my back, I'll come in and set."

Tyrel got up. "Tell . . . I'll be damned."

"Likely," I said, "but don't blame it on me. When I rode off to the wars I left you in good hands."

Turning toward Tyrel's wife, a lovely, dark-eyed, dark-haired girl who looked like a princess out of a book, I said, "Ma'am, I'm William Tell Sackett, and you'll be Drusilla, my brother's wife."

She put her hands on mine and stood on tiptoe and kissed me, and my face colored up and I went hot clean to my boots. Tyrel laughed, and then he looked past me into the darkness and said, "It's all right, Cap. This is my brother Tell."

He came in out of the darkness then, a thin old man with cold gray eyes and a gray mustache above a hard mouth. There was no give to this man, I figured. Had I been a wrong one I would have been killed.

We shook hands and neither of us said anything. Cap was not a talkative man, and I am only at times.

Ma turned her head. "Juana, come get my son his supper."

I couldn't believe it—Ma with household help. Long as I could recall, nobody had done for us boys but Ma herself, working early and late and never complaining.

Juana was a Mexican-Indian girl and she brought the food in fancy plates. I looked at it and commenced to feel mighty uncomfortable. I'd not eaten a meal in the presence of a woman for a long time, and was embarrassed and worried. I'd no idea how to eat proper. In a trail camp a body eats because he's hungry and doesn't think much of the way he does it.

"If it's all the same to you," I said, "I'll go outside. Under a roof like this I'm mighty skittish."

Drusilla took my sleeve and led me to the chair. "You sit down, Tell. And don't you worry. We want you to eat with us and we want you to tell us what you've been doing."

First I thought of that gold.

I went out and fetched it. Putting my saddlebags down on the table, I took out a chunk of the gold, still grainy with quartz fragments, but gold.

It shook them. Nothing, I'd figured, would ever shake Tyrel, but this did.

While they looked at the gold I went to the kitchen and washed my hands in a big basin and dried them on a white towel.

Everything was spotless and clean. The floor was like the deck of a steamboat I traveled on one time on the Mississippi. It was the kind of living I'd always wanted for Ma, but I'd had no hand in this. Orrin and Tyrel had done it.

While I ate, I told them about the gold. I'd taken a big slab of bread and buttered it liberal, and I ate it in two bites, while talking and drinking coffee. First real butter I'd tasted in more than a year, and the first real coffee in longer than that.

Through the open door into the parlor I could see furniture made of some dark wood, and shelves with books. While they talked, I got up and went in there, taking the lamp along. I squatted on my heels to look at the books, fair hungering for them. I taken one down and turned the leaves real slow, careful not to dirty them, and tested the weight of the book in my hand. A book as heavy as one of these, I figured, must make a lot of sense.

I rested a finger on a line of print and tried to get the way of it, but there were words I'd never seen before. Back to home we'd had no books but an almanac and the Bible.

There was a book there by a man named Blackstone, seemed to be about the law, and several others. I felt a longing in me to read them all, to know them, to have them always at my hand. I looked through book after book, and sometimes I would find a word I could recognize, or even a sentence I could make out.

Such words would catch my eye like a deer taking off into the woods or the sudden lift of a gun barrel in the sun. One place I found something I puzzled out, and I do not know why it was this I chose. It was from Blackstone.

"... that the whole should protect all its parts, and that every part should pay obedience to the will of the whole; or, in other words, that the community should guard the rights of each individual member, and that (in return for this protection) each individual should submit to the laws of the community; without which submission of all it was impossible that protection could be extended to any."

It took me a spell, working that out in my mind, to get the sense of it. Yet somehow it stayed with me, and in the days to come I thought it over a good bit.

Returning the books to their places, I stood up, and I looked around very carefully. This was Ma's home, and it was Tyrel's and Orrin's. It was not mine.

They had earned it with their hands and with their knowing ways, and they had given this place to Ma.

Tyrel was no longer the lean, hungry mountain boy. He stood tall now, and carried himself very straight and with a kind of style. He wore a black broadcloth coat and a white shirt like a man born to them and, come to think of it, he was even better-looking than Orrin.

I stared at myself in the mirror. No getting around it, I was a homely man. Over-tall and mighty little meat, with a big-boned face like a wedge. There was an old scar on my cheekbone from a cutting scrape in New Orleans. My shoulders were heavy with muscle, but a mite stooped. In my wore-out army shirt and cow-country jeans I didn't come to much.

My brothers were younger than me, and probably brighter. Hands and a strong back were all I had. I could move almost anything I put a hand to, and I could ride and rope, but what was that?

My mind turned back to that passage in the book. There was the kind of rule for men to live by. I'd no idea such things were written down in books.

Orrin had come while I was inside, and he'd taken his gee-tar and was singing. He sang "Black, Black, Black," "Barb'ry Allen," and "The Golden Vanity."

It was like old times ... only it wasn't old times and the boys had left me far, far behind. Twenty-eight years old in a few days—with years of brute hard living behind me—but if Orrin and Tyrel could do it, I was going to try.

Come daylight, I was going to shape my way for the mountains, for the high far valley, and the stream. First I must sell my gold and buy an outfit. Then I would light out. And it was best I go soon, for the Bigelows might come hunting me. Turned out less simple than that.

Las Vegas was the nearest place I could get the kind of outfit I wanted. We hitched up, Tyrel and me, and we drove down to Las Vegas with Cap riding horseback along with us. That old coot was a man to ride the river with, believe me.

"Wherever you go," Cap told me, "if you show that gold you'll empty the town. They'll foller you . . . they'll track you down, and if they get a chance, they'll kill you. That's the strike of a lifetime."

Riding to Las Vegas I got an idea. Somewhere on that stream that ran down from the mountains I would stake a claim, and folks would think the gold came from *that* claim and never look for the other.

"You do that," Cap's old eyes twinkled a mite, "and I'll give you a name for it. You can call it the Red Herring."

When I showed my gold in the bank at Las Vegas the man behind the wicket turned a little pale around the eyes, and I knew what Cap Rountree had said was truth. If ever there was greed in a man's eyes, it was in his. "Where did you get this gold?" he demanded.

"Mister," I said, "if you want to buy it, quote me a price. Otherwise I'll go elsewhere."

He was a tall, thin man with sharp gray eyes that seemed to have only a black speck for a pupil. He had a thin face and a carefully trimmed mustache.

He touched his tongue to his lips and lifted those eyes to me. "It might be st——"

When he saw the look in my eyes he stopped, and just at that moment, Tyrel and Orrin came in. Orrin had come down earlier than we had for some business. They walked over.

"Is anything wrong, Tell?"

"Not yet," I said.

"Oh, Orrin." The banker's eyes flickered to Tyrel and back to me. The family resemblance was strong.

"I was about to buy some gold. A brother of yours?"

"Tell, this is John Tuthill."

"It is always a pleasure to meet one of the Sackett family," Tuthill said, but when our eyes met we both knew it was no pleasure at all. For either of us.

"My brother has just come down from Montana," Orrin said smoothly. "He's been mining up there."

"He looks like a cattleman."

"I have been, and will be again."

After that we shopped around, buying me an outfit. There was no gainsaying the fact that I'd need a pick and a shovel, a single-jack, and some drills. That is mining equipment in any man's figuring, and there was no way of sidestepping it. I'm not overly suspicious, but no man ever lost his hair by being careful, and I kept an eye on my back trail as we roamed about town.

After a while Tyrel and Orrin went about their business and I finished getting my outfit together. Cap was nowhere to be seen, but he needed no keeper. Cap had been up the creek and over the mountain in his time. Anybody who latched onto that old man latched onto trouble.

Dark came on. I left my gear at the livery stable and started up the street. I paused to look over toward the mountains and I got a look behind me. Sure enough, I'd picked up an Indian.

Only he was no Indian, he was a slick-looking party who seemed to have nothing to do but keep an eye on me. Right away it came to mind that he might be a Bigelow, so I just turned down an alley and walked slow.

He must have been afraid I would get away from him, for he came running, and I did a boxer's sidestep into the shadows. My sudden disappearance must have surprised him. He skidded to a stop, and when he stopped I hit him.

My fists are big, and my hands are work-hardened. When I connected with his jaw it sounded like the butt end of an axe hitting a log.

Anybody who figures to climb my frame is somebody I wish to know better, so I took him by the shirt-front with my left hand and dragged him into the saloon where I was to meet the boys.

Folks looked up, always interested in something coming off, so I taken a better grip and one-handed him to a seat on the bar.

"I hadn't baited no hook, but this gent's been bobbin' my cork," I said. "Any of you know him? He just tried to jump me in the alley."

"That's Will Boyd. He's a gambler."

"He put his money on the wrong card," I said. "I don't like being followed down alleys."

Boyd was coming out of it, and when he realized where he was he started to slide down off the bar, only I held him fast. From my belt scabbard I took that Arkansas toothpick of mine, which I use for any manner of things.

"You have been led upon evil ways," I explained, "and the way of the transgressor is hard. Seems to me the thing led you down the wrong road is that mustache."

He was looking at me with no favor, and I knew he was one man would try to kill me first chance he had. He was a man with a lot to learn, and he wouldn't learn it any younger.

Balancing that razor-sharp knife in my hand I said, "You take this knife, and you shave off that mustache."

He didn't believe me. You could see he just couldn't believe this could be happening to him. He didn't even want to believe it, so I explained.

"You come hunting me," I said, "and I'm a mild man who likes to be left alone. You need something to remind you of the error of your ways."

So I held out the knife to him, haft first, and I could see him wondering if he dared try to run it into me. "Mister, don't make me lose my patience. If I do I'll whup you."

He took the knife, carefully, because he didn't feel lucky, and he started on that mustache. It was a stiff mustache and he had no water and no soap and, mister, it hurt.

"Next time you start down an alley after a man, you stop and think about it."

I heard the saloon door close. Boyd's eyes flickered. He started to speak, then shut up. The man was John Tuthill.

"Here!" His voice had authority. "What's going on?"

"Man shaving a mustache," I said. "He decided

he'd rather shave it than otherwise." Turning my eyes momentarily, I said, "How about you? You want to shave, Mr. Tuthill?"

His face turned pink as a baby's, then he said, "If that man did something unlawful, have him arrested."

"You'd send a man to *prison*?" Seemed like I was mighty upset. "That's awful! You'd imprison a fellowman?"

Nobody around seemed likely to side him and he shut up, but he didn't like it. Seemed likely he was the man who set Boyd to following me, but I had no proof.

Boyd was making rough work of the shaving, hacking away at it, and in places his lip was raw. "When he gets through," I said, "he's leaving town. If he ever finds himself in another town where I am, he'll ride out of that one too."

By sunup the story was all over town, or so I heard—I wasn't there. I was on my way back to Mora, riding with Tyrel and Cap.

Orrin followed us by several hours, and when he came into the yard in the buckboard Cap was watching me arrange my gear in bundles.

"If you're a man who likes company," Cap said, "I'm a man to ride the hills. I'm getting cabin fever."

"Pleased," I said. "Pleased to have you."

Orrin got down from the buckboard and walked over. "By the way, Tell. There was a man in Las Vegas inquiring for you. Said his name was Bigelow."

CHAPTER 5

WE STARTED UP Coyote Creek in the late hours of night, with the stars hanging their bright lanterns over the mountains. Cap was riding point, our six packhorses trailing him, and me riding drag. A chill wind came down off the Sangre de Cristos, and somewhere out over the bottom a quail was calling.

Cap had a sour, dry-mouthed look to him. He was the kind if you got in trouble you didn't look to see if he was still with you—you knew damned well he was.

Not wishing to be seen leaving, we avoided Mora, and unless somebody was lying atop that rocky ridge near the ranch it was unlikely that we were seen.

The Mora River flowed through a narrow gap at the ranch and out into the flatlands beyond, and we had only to follow the Mora until it was joined by Coyote Creek, then turned up Coyote and across the wide valley of La Cueva.

We circled around the sleeping village of Golondrinos, and pointed north, shivering in the morning cold. The sky was stark and clear, the ridges sharply cut against the faintly lightening sky. Grass swished about our horses' hoofs, our saddles creaked, and over at Golondrinos a dog barked inquiringly into the morning.

Cap Rountree hunched his shoulders in his wore-out homespun coat and never once looked back to see if we were coming along. He did his part and expected others to do theirs.

I had a lot to think about, and there's no better time for thinking than a day in the saddle. There'd been many changes in life for Orrin and Tyrel and Ma, and my mind was full of them.

I had rolled out of my soogan at three o'clock that morning. It was cold, believe me. Any time you think summer is an always warm time, you try a high country in the Southwest with mountains close by.

After rolling my bed for travel, I went down to the corral, shook out a loop, and caught up the horses. They were frosty and wild-eyed and suspected my notions, liking their corral.

Before there was a light in the house I had those horses out and tied to the corral with their pack saddles on them. Then I stepped into the leather on my appaloosa to top him off and get the kinks out of him. By the time I had him stopped pitching and bucking, Cap was around.

The door opened, throwing a rectangle of light into the yard. It was Drusilla, Tyrel's wife. "Come and get it," she said, and I never heard a prettier sound.

Cap and me, we came in out of the dark, our guns belted on, and wearing jackets. We hung our hats on pegs and rinsed our hands off in the wash basin. Cap had a face on that would sour milk.

Tyrel was at table, fresh-shaved and looking fit as a man could. How he found the time, I didn't know, but sizing him up, I decided it was mighty becoming in a man to be fresh-shaved at breakfast. Seemed like if I was going to fit myself for living with a woman I'd have to tone up my manners.

Womenfolks were something I'd seen little of, and having them around was unsettling, sort of. But I could see the advantages. It's a comforting thing to hear a woman about tinkling dishes, and stepping light, and looking pretty.

Ma was up, too. She was no youngster any more, and some crippled by rheumatism, but Ma would never be abed when one of us boys was taking off. The room was warm from the fire and there was a fine smell of bacon frying and coffee steaming. Drusilla had been raised right. She had a mug of steaming coffee before Cap and me as soon as we set down to table.

Drusilla looked slim and pretty as a three-month-old fawn, her eyes big and dark and warm. That Tyrel was a lucky man.

Cap was a good eater and he leaned into his food. I ate seven eggs, nine strips of bacon and six hot-cakes, and drank five cups of coffee. Tyrel watched me, no smile on his face. Then he looked over at Dru. "I'd sooner buy his clothes than feed him," he said.

Finally I got up and took up my Winchester. At the door I stopped and looked at Ma, then around the room. It was warm, comfortable, friendly. It was home. Ma'd never had much until now, and what she had now wasn't riches, but it was better than ever before, and she was happy. The boys had done well by her, and well by themselves.

Me? The least I could do was try to make something of myself. The eldest-born, the last to amount to anything, if ever.

Tyrel came outside when I stepped into the saddle and handed me up that copy of Blackstone he'd seen me looking at. "Give it study, Tell," he said. "It's the law we live by, and a lot of men did a lot of thinking for a lot of years to make it so."

I'd never owned a book before, or had the loan of one, but it was a friendly feeling, knowing it was there in my saddlebag, waiting to give me its message over a lot of campfires to come.

The proper route to the country where we were headed was up the old Spanish Trail, but Cap suggested we head north for San Luis and old Fort Massachusetts, to avoid anybody who might be laying for us. We made camp that night in the pines a half-mile back from Black Lake.

Earlier, we had ridden through the village of Guadalupita without stopping. In a country where folks are few they make up for it with curiosity. News is a scarce thing in the far hills. Two men riding north with six packhorses were bound to cause comment.

It was a quiet night, and we weren't to see too many of that kind for a long, long time.

Coyotes talked inquiringly to the moon and cocked their ears for the echo of their own voices. Somewhere up the slope an old grizzly poked around in the brush, but he paid us no mind, muttering to himself like a grouchy old man.

About the time coffee water was on, Cap opened up and started to talk. He had his pipe going and I had some steaks broiling.

"Coolest man I ever saw in a difficulty is your brother Tyrel. Only time he had me worried was when he faced up to Tom Sunday.

"You've heard tell of Sunday? He was our friend. As good a man as ever stretched a buffalo hide, but when Orrin commenced getting the things Tom Sunday figured should come to him, trouble showed its hand.

"Sunday was a big, handsome, laughing man, a man of education and background, but hell on wheels in any kind of a fight. Only when Orrin edged him out on things, though Orrin wanted to share everything, or even step aside for him, Tom turned mean and Tye had to get tough with him."

"Tye's a good man with a gun."

"Shooting's the least of it," Cap said irritably. "Any man can shoot a gun, and with practice he can draw fast and shoot accurately, but that makes no difference. What counts is how you stand up when somebody is shooting back at you."

I hadn't heard Cap talk much before but Tyrel was one of his few enthusiasms, and I could see why.

———

GOLD IS A hard-kept secret.

The good, the bad, the strong, and the weak all flock to the kind of warmth that gold gives off.

Come daylight we moved out, and soon we had Angel Fire Mountain abreast of us, with Old Taos Pass cutting into the hills ahead and on our left. Cap was troubled in his mind about our back trail, and he was giving it attention.

Wind was talking in the pines along the long slopes

when we rode into the high valley called Eagle Nest. The trail to Cimarron cut off into the mountains east of us, so I broke away from the pack train and scouted the ground where the trail came out into the valley. Several lone riders and at least one party had headed north toward Elizabethtown.

We hauled rein and contemplated. We could follow Moreno Creek right into town, or we could cut around a mountain by following Comanche Creek, but it would be better to seem unconcerned and to ride right on into town and stop for a meal, giving out that we were bound up the trail for Idaho where I had a claim.

Elizabethtown was still a supply point for a few prospectors working the hills, and a rough crowd, left over from the Land Grant fighting, hung out there. We turned our stock into an abandoned corral and paid a Mexican to look after them and our outfits.

As we walked toward the nearest bar Cap told me that eight or ten men had been killed in there, and I could see why. There was twenty feet of bar in forty feet of room. The range was so short that a man could scarcely miss.

"The grub's good," Cap said. "They've got a cook who used to be chef in a big hotel back east—until he killed a man and had to light out."

The men at the bar were a rugged lot, which meant nothing, for good men can look as rough as bad men, and often do.

"The one with the General Grant beard," Cap commented, "that's Ben Hobes . . . he's on the wanted list in Texas."

The bartender came over. "What's it for you?" He glanced at Cap Rountree. "Ain't seen you in a while."

"And you won't," Cap said, "not unless you come to Idaho. We got us a claim. . . . Who's that white-headed kid at the bar with Ben?"

The bartender shrugged. "Drifter . . . figures he should be considered a bad man. I ain't seen any graveyards yet."

"You got some of those oysters? Fix me up a stew."

"Same for me," I said, "only twice as much, and a chunk of beef, if you've got it."

"Cookie's got a roast on—best you ever ate."

The bartender walked away, and Cap said, "Sam's all right. He's neutral, the way he should be. Wants no trouble."

The white-headed kid that Cap had asked about leaned his elbows on the bar, hooking a heel over the brass rail. He was wearing two guns, tied down. He had a long, thin face, his eyes were close-set, and there was a twist to his mouth.

He said something to Ben Hobes, and the older man said, "Forget it." Cap looked at me, his eyes grim.

After a few minutes the bartender came in with the grub and we started to eat. Cap was right. This man could sure put the groceries together.

"He can cook, all right," I said to Cap. "How'd he kill that man?"

"Poisoned him," Cap said, and grinned at me.

CHAPTER 6

WE WERE HUNGRY. Nobody savors his own cooking too much, and in the months to come we figured to have too much of ours, so we enjoyed that meal. Whatever else the cook was, he understood food.

All the time there was talk at the bar. Folks who live quiet in well-ordered communities probably never face up to such a situation. It was a time of free-moving, independent men, each jealous of his own pride, and touchy on points that everybody is touchy about.

And there are always those who want to be thought big men, who want to walk with great strides across the world, be pointed out, and looked up to. Trouble is, they all don't have what it takes to be like that.

Up there at the bar was this white-headed young-ster they were calling Kid Newton, feeling his oats and wanting to stack up against somebody. Cap could see it just as I could; and Ben Hobes, who stood up there beside him, was made nervous by it.

Ben Hobes was a hard man. Nobody needed to point that out, but a man should be wary of the company he keeps, because a trouble-hunter can get you into a bind you'd never get into by yourself. And that Kid Newton was hunting a handle for trouble. He wanted it, and wanted it bad, feeling if he could kill somebody folks would look up to him. And we were strangers.

The thing wrong with strangers, you never know who they are. Cap now, he was a thin old man, and to Newton he might look like somebody to ride over, instead of an old buffalo hunter and Indian fighter who'd seen a hundred youngsters like Kid Newton get taken down.

Me, I'm so tall and thin for my height (Ma says I should put on thirty pounds) that he might figure me as nothing to worry about.

Trouble was the last thing I wanted. Back in Uvalde I'd killed Bigelow in a showdown I couldn't get out of any other way—unless I wanted to die. That was likely to give me all the difficulty I'd want.

Newton was looking at Cap. He grinned, and I heard Hobes say again, "Forget it."

"Aw, what's the matter?" I heard the Kid say, "I'm just gonna have some fun." Ben whispered to him, but the Kid paid him no mind.

"Hey, old man! Ain't you kind of old to be traipsin' over the country?"

Cap didn't even look up, although the lines in his face deepened a little. I reached down real slow and taken my pistol out and laid it on the table. I mean I taken one pistol out. I was wearing another in my waistband.

When I put that pistol on the table beside my plate, the Kid looked over at me, and so did Ben Hobes. He threw me a sharp look, and kind of half squared around toward us. Me, I didn't say anything or look around. I just kept eating.

The Kid looked at the gun and he looked at me. "What's that for?"

Surprised-like, I looked up. "What's what for?"

"The gun."

"Oh? *That?* That's for killing varmints, snakes, coyotes, and such-like. Sometimes frogs."

"You aimin' that at me?" He was really asking for it.

"Why, now. Why would I do a thing like that? A nice boy like you." He was young enough to get mad at being called a boy, but he couldn't make up his mind whether I was makin' fun, or what.

"I'll bet you got a home somewheres, and a mother." I looked at him thoughtfully. "Why, sure! I see no reason . . . *exactly,* why you shouldn't have a mother like anybody else."

Taking a big bite of bread, I chewed it for a minute while he was thinking of something to say. I waited until he was ready to say it and then said, "You had your supper, son? Why don't you set down here with us and have a bite? And when you go out of a night you should bundle up more. A body could catch his death of cold."

He was mad now, but ashamed, too. Everybody was starting to smile a little. He dearly wanted a fight, but it's pretty hard to draw a gun on a man who's worried about your welfare.

"Here . . ." I pushed back a chair. "Come and set down. No doubt you've been long from home, and your mama is worried about you. Maybe you feel troubled in your mind, so you just set up and tell us about it. After you've had something to eat, you'll feel better."

Whatever he had fixed to say didn't fit any more, and he groped for words and finally said, "I'm not hungry."

"Don't be bashful, son. We've got a-plenty. Cap here . . . he has youngsters like you . . . he must have, he's been gallopin' around over the country so much. He must have left some like you somewhere."

Somebody laughed out loud, and the Kid stiffened up. "What do you mean by that?" His voice shrilled a little, and that made him still madder. "Damn you—"

"Bartender," I said, "why don't you fix this boy a little warm broth? Something that will rest easy on his stomach?"

Pushing back my chair, I got up and holstered my gun. Cap got up, too, and I handed the bartender the money, then added an extra quarter. "This is for the broth. Make it hot, now."

Turning around, I looked at the Kid mildly and held out my hand. "Good-bye, son. Walk in the ways of righteousness, and don't forget your mother's teaching."

Almost automatically he took my hand, then jerked his back like it was bee-stung.

Cap had started toward the door, and I followed him. At the door I turned and looked back at the Kid again. I've got big eyes and they are serious most times. This time I tried to make them especially serious. "But really, son, you should bundle up more."

Then I stepped outside and we walked back to our outfit. I said to Cap. "You tired?"

"No," he said, "and a few miles will do us no harm."

We rode out. Couple of times I caught Cap sizing

me up, like, but he said nothing at all. Not for several miles, anyway, then he asked, "You realize you called that boy a bastard?"

"Well, now. That's strong language, Cap, and I never use strong language."

"You talked him out of it. You made him look the fool."

"A soft answer turneth away wrath," I said. "Or that's what the Good Book says."

We rode on for a couple of long hours and then camped in the woods on Comanche Creek, bedding down for a good rest.

We slept past daylight and took our time when we did get up, so we could watch our trail and see if anybody was behind us.

About an hour past daylight we saw a half-dozen riders going north. If they were following us, they did not see our tracks. We had made our turn in the creek bottom, and by this time any tracks left there had washed away.

It was on to midday before we started out, and we held close to the east side of the valley where we could lose our shape against the background of trees, rocks, and brush. We were over nine thousand feet up, and here the air was cool by day and right cold by night.

We cut across the sign of those riders and took the trail along Costilla Creek, and up through the canyon. At Costilla Creek the riders had turned right on the most obvious trail, but Cap said there was an old Indian trail up Costilla, and we took it.

We rode into San Luis late in the afternoon. It was a pleasant little town where the folks were all of

Spanish descent. We corralled our stock, hiring a man to watch over our gear again. Then we walked over to Salazar's store. Folks all over this part of the country came there for supplies and news. A family named Gallegos had founded that store many years back, and later this Salazar took it over.

These were friendly, peaceful folks. They had settled in here years before, and were making a good thing of it. We were buying a few things when all of a sudden a woman's voice said, "Señor?"

We turned around; she was speaking to Cap. Soon as he saw her, he said, "Buenos dias, Tina. It has been a long time."

He turned to me. "Tina, this is Tell Sackett, Tyrel's brother."

She was a pretty little woman with great big eyes. "How do you do, Señor? I owe your brother much thanks. He helped me when I had need."

"He's a good man."

"Si . . . he is."

We talked a mite, and then a slender whip of a Mexican with high cheekbones and very black eyes came in. He was not tall, and he wouldn't have weighed any more than Cap, but it took only a glance to see he was mucho hombre.

"It is my hoosband, Esteban Mendoza." She spoke quickly to him in Spanish, explaining who we were. His eyes warmed and he held out his hand.

We had dinner that night with Tina and Esteban, a quiet dinner, in a little adobe house with a string of red peppers hanging on the porch. Inside there was a black-eyed baby with round cheeks and a quick smile.

Esteban was a *vaquero,* or had been. He had also driven a freight team over the road to Del Norte.

"Be careful," he warned. "There is much trouble in the San Juans and Uncomphagre. Clint Stockton is there, with his outlaws."

"Any drifters riding through?" Cap asked.

Esteban glanced at him shrewdly. "Si. Six men were here last night. One was a square man with a beard. Another"—Esteban permitted himself a slight smile, revealing beautiful teeth and a sly amusement—"another had two pistols."

"Six, you said?"

"There were six. Two of them were larger than you, Señor Tell, very broad, powerful. Big blond men with small eyes and big jaws. One of them, I think, was the leader."

"Know them?" Cap asked me.

"No, Cap, I don't." Yet even as I said it, I began to wonder. What did the Bigelows look like?

I asked Esteban, "Did you hear any names?"

"No, Señor. They talked very little. Only to ask about travelers."

They must know that either we were behind them, or had taken another trail. Why were they following us, if they were?

The way west after leaving Del Norte lay through the mountains, over Wolf Creek Pass. This was a high, narrow, twisting pass that was most difficult to travel, a very bad place to run into trouble.

It was a pleasant evening, and it did me good to see the nice home the Mendozas had here, the baby, and their pleasure in being together. But the thought of those six men and why they were riding after us worried me, and I could see Cap had it in mind.

We saddled up and got moving. During the ride west Cap Rountree, who had lived among Indians for years, told me more about them than I'd ever expected to know. This was Ute country, though the Comanches had intruded into some of it. A warlike tribe, they had been pushed out of the Black Hills by the Sioux and had come south, tying up with the still more warlike and bloody Kiowa. Cap said that the Kiowa had killed more whites than any other tribe.

At first the Utes and the Comanches, both of Shoshone ancestry, had got along all right. Later they split and were often at war. Before the white man came the Indians were continually at war with one another, except for the Iroquois in the East, who conquered an area bigger than the Roman empire and then made a peace that lasted more than a hundred years.

Cap and I rode through some of the wildest and most beautiful country under the sun, following the Rio Grande up higher and still higher into the mountains. It was hard to believe this was the same river along which I'd fought Comanches and outlaws in Texas—that we camped of a night beside water that would run into the Gulf one day.

Night after night our smoke lifted to the stars from country where we found no tracks. Still, cold, and aloof, the snow-capped peaks lifted above us. Cap, he was a changed man, gentler, somehow, and of a night he talked like he'd never done down below. And sometimes I opened up my Blackstone and read, smelling the smoke of aspen and cedar, smelling the pines, feeling the cold wind off the high snow.

It was like that until we came down Bear Creek into the canyon of the Vallecitos.

West of us rose up the high peaks of the Grenadier and Needle Mountains of the San Juan range. We pulled up by a stream that ran cold and swift from the mountains. Looking up at the peaks I wondered again: what was it up there that got the meat I left hanging in that tree?

Cap, he taken a pan and went down to the creek. In the late evening he washed it out and came back to the fire.

There were flecks of gold in the pan . . . we'd found color. Here we would stake our claim.

CHAPTER 7

WE FORTED UP for trouble.

Men most likely had been following us. Sooner or later they would find us, and we could not be sure of their intentions. Moreover, the temper of the Utes was never too certain a thing.

Riding up there, I'd had time for thinking. Where gold was found, men would come.

There would be trouble—we expected that—but there would be business too. The more I thought, the more it seemed to me that the man who had something to sell would be better off than a man who searched for gold.

We had made camp alongside a spring not far from the plunging stream that came down the mountainside and emptied into the Vallecitos. I was sure this was the stream I had followed into the high valley where my gold was. Our camp was on a long bench above the Vallecitos, with the mountainside rising steeply behind it and to the east. We were in a clump of scattered ponderosa pine and Douglas fir.

First, we shook out our loops and snaked some deadfall logs into spaces between the trees. Next we made a corral by cutting some lodgepole pine—the lodgepole pine grew mostly, it seemed, in areas that had been burned over—and laying the ends of the poles in tree forks or lashing them to trees with rawhide. It was hard work, but we both knew what needed to be done and there was little talk and no waste effort.

Short of sundown I walked out of the trees and along the bench. Looking north, we faced the widest spot we had so far seen in the canyon of the Vallecitos. It was a good mile north of our camp.

"That's where we'll build the town," I told Cap.

He took his pipe out of his mouth. "Town?"

"Where there's gold, there'll be folks. Where folks are, there's wanting. I figure we can set up store and supply those wants. Whether they find gold or not, they will be eating and needing tools, powder, blankets—all that sort of thing. It seems to be the surest way, Cap, if a man wants to make him a living. Gold is found and is mined, but the miners eat."

"You won't find me tending store," Cap said.

"Me, neither. But we'll lay out the town site, you and me. We'll stake the lots, and we'll watch for a good man. Believe me, he'll come along. Then we'll set him up in business."

"You Sacketts," Cap said, "sure play hell once you get out of the mountains. Only thing puzzles me is, what kept you there so long?"

The next few days we worked sunrise to sundown. We paced off a street maybe four hundred yards long, we laid out lots, and planned the town. We figured on a general store, a livery stable, a hotel and boarding house, and two saloons. We spotted a place for a blacksmith shop, and for an assayer.

We cut logs and dragged some of them down to the site for the store, and we put up signs indicating that any folks who came along were to see us about the lots.

Meantime, we worked a little on the claim—rarely more than a pan or two a day because we had much else to do. But we found color—not a lot, but some.

We also improved our fort. Not that it looked much like one, and we didn't want it to, but we were set up to fight off an attack if it came.

Neither one of us had much trust in the peaceful qualities of our fellowmen. Seems to me most of the folks doing all the talk about peace and giving the other fellow the benefit of the doubt were folks setting back to home in cushy chairs with plenty of grub around and the police nearby to protect them. Back there, men would set down safe of an evening and write about how cruel the poor Indian was being treated out west. They never come upon the body of a friend who had been staked out on an ant hill or had a fire built on his stomach, nor had they stood off a charge of Indians.

Personally, I found Indians people to respect. Their ways weren't our ways, and a lot of virtues they were given credit for by white men were only ideas in a white man's head, and no Indian would have considered them virtues. Mercy rarely had any part in the makeup of an Indian.

Folks talk about human nature, but what they mean is not human nature, but the way they are brought up. It seems to me that folks who are brought up to Christian ways of thought don't believe in the taking of life, but the Indian had no such conception. If you were a stranger you were an enemy. If you gave him gifts it was usually because you were afraid of him . . . or that's how he thought.

Indians were fighting men. Fighting was their greatest sport and occupation. Our people look up to athletes of one kind or another, but the Indian saved all his respect for fighting men. And an Indian would count the scalp of a woman or a child as well as a man's.

This was wrong to our way of thinking, but his thinking was altogether different.

The Indian, before the white man took up the West, was physically cleaner than the white man. He bathed often, and it wasn't until white man's liquor and poverty caught up with him that he lost the old ways. But the Indian warrior would have been ashamed of all the milksop talk about the poor Indian. He was strong, he was proud, and he was able to handle his own problems.

————

IT WAS SUNDAY before trouble showed. Sunday was a quiet time for us. Cap was busy scraping and tanning some elk and deer hides, and after cleaning my weapons and catching a bait of trout, I settled down to study Blackstone.

It was a warm, lazy day, with sunlight sparkling on the creek waters, and scarce a breeze stirring the pines overhead. Time to time my thoughts would drift from my study to that high valley. If I wanted to go up and get some of that gold I would have to find another way into that valley before snow fell and closed it off.

"Tell . . ."

Cap spoke softly, and I got up and walked over to

him. He was looking off through the trees, and we could see four riders over by the town site. They turned toward us, and I got out my field glass. There was nothing familiar about any of them. While I watched they started in our direction, and the last man in line checked his pistol.

Down the bench, maybe fifty yards or so, they slowed to a stop, seeing the corral with the horses in it, and the smoke from our fire. Then they came on up.

Me, I was wearing an old U.S. Army hat, a wore-out blue army shirt and jeans, and I had me a belt gun on. When I sighted them coming I taken up my Winchester, and Cap and me stood out to greet them.

" 'Light," I said. "Ain't often we have visitors."

"Looks of that town site, you must be expectin' plenty," one of them said. "What would a man want with a town here?"

"Well, sir," I said, "we took a notion. Cap Rountree an' me, we like to go to town of an evening when the chores are done. There ain't no town close up, so we decided to build our own. We laid her out and started cuttin' timber. Then we held an election."

"An *election?*"

"Town ought to have a mayor. We elected Cap by acclamation. Cap never has been a mayor before, and the town never had one. We figured they could start off together."

While I was talking, I was looking them over. One was riding a horse branded with a pitchfork over a bar. The owner used to call it the Pitchfork Bar, but folks who knew the ways of the outfit called it the Fork Over, because that was what you had to do if you crossed their range. The man on this horse was a big man with a wide face and thick, blond hair. He kept staring at me, and at what remained of my uniform.

There was a stoop-shouldered man with narrow black eyes, and a square-set one with an open, friendly face, and a fat man with a round face—round and mighty hard.

"You must be proud of that uniform," the big one said. "The war's been over a long time."

"Ain't had money enough to shed it," I said.

The fat man walked his horse toward the creek, then called back, "Kitch, lookit here!"

They all rode over, and Cap and me followed.

Kitch looked over our shaft, which was only down a few feet. "Gold?" He was amazed "This here's silver country."

"Spot of color," I said. "Nothing much yet, but we've got hopes."

The fat man paid us no mind. "Kitch," he said, "they've got a good thing here. That's why they've laid out the town. Once folks hear of a strike, they'll come running, and that town will be a gold mine itself."

"Only there hasn't been any strike," Cap said. "We're scarcely making wages."

He turned and walked off, saying, "I'll put some coffee on, Tell."

At the name, Kitch turned sharply around and looked at me. "Tell? Are you Tell Sackett?"

"Uh-huh."

He chuckled. "Mister, you're going to have company. Seen a couple of men in Silverton who were hunting you."

"I'll be here."

"They tell me you can sure run." Kitch had a mean look to his eyes. "I seen many a-running with that uniform on."

"All the way to Lee's surrender," I said. "We stopped running then."

He started to say something and his face hardened up and he commenced getting red around the gills.

"The Bigelows say every time you get stopped somewhere they come along and you take out like a scared rabbit."

Tell Sackett, I told myself, *this man aims to get you into a fight. Have no part of it.* "Any man who wants to kill me," I said, "can do it on his own time. I got too many things to do to waste time."

Cap was back behind the logs near the fire, and I knew what he would be doing back there.

"Now I tell you what you do," I said. "You go back to Silverton and you tell the Bigelow boys I'm here. You tell them their brother tried dealing off the bottom with the wrong man, and if they're of a mind to, they can find me here. This is as far as I'm going."

I added, more quietly, "And, Kitch, you said something about running. You come back with them. I'll be right here."

Kitch was startled, then angry. But the fat man spoke up. "Let's get out of here."

They started off. Only the square-built man lingered. "Mr. Sackett, I'd like to come back and talk to you, if I may."

"Any time," I said, and he rode off.

W E WORKED OUR claim, got out some gold, and built a rocker. Meanwhile I cut a hidden trail up the steep mountainside behind our camp. About two hundred feet above, covering the bench, I built a rifle-pit of brush, deadfalls, and rocks—a shelter where two or three men could cover all approaches to our camp.

The following day, switching back and forth to make it an easier climb, I opened a way further up the ridge.

"What's the idea?" Cap asked me, come nightfall.

"If I have to start running," I said, "I don't want anything in the way. I've got big feet."

Over the fire that night, Cap looked at me.

"When you going back up on that mountain?"

"And leave you with trouble shaping up?"

"Forget it. Trouble is no stranger to me. You go ahead, only don't be gone too long."

I told him I didn't know exactly how to get up there from where we were. We were close, that much I knew.

Cap said the way I came before, judging from my description, had brought me over Columbine Pass and up to the Vallecitos along Johnson Creek. That was south of us, so if I rode south I might recognize something or come on one of the markers.

The idea of leaving Cap alone worried me. Sure, he was an old wolf, but I had many enemies around, what with the Bigelows, Ben Hobes, and that white-haired kid with the two guns. To say nothing of Tuthill, back in Las Vegas, and his gambler friend.

Trouble just naturally seemed to latch onto me and hang on with all its teeth.

On the other hand, Cap had plenty of ca'tridges, he had meat, and there was a spring. Unless they caught him away from camp he could stand off a good-sized force, and we were not expecting anything of the kind.

From worrying about Cap, I turned to thinking back to home, and Tyrel and Dru. It was a fine thing for a man to have a woman love him like that, a fine thing. But who would I ever find? It was complete and total unlikely that any female woman in her right mind would fall into love with the likes of me. It was likely all I'd ever have would be a horse and maybe a dog.

Lying there, I could smell the smoke of the dying fire, see the stars through the tops of the pines, and hear the wind along the ranges. The moon came up and, off to the west, I could see the towering, snow-capped peaks of the Needle Mountains.

Suddenly I sat up. "Cap!" I whispered. "You hear that?"

"I hear it."

"Sounds like somebody crying." I got up and pulled on my boots. The sound had died away, but it seemed to have come from somewhere upwind of us.

We walked to the edge of the trees and listened, but we heard it no more. Putting my hands to my mouth, I called, not too loud. "Come on into camp! No use to be out there alone!"

"How do you know it's alone?" Cap asked mildly. "Come on back to sleep. You believe in ha'nts? A trick of the wind, that's all."

I heard no further sound, so I followed Cap and turned in. And, although I lay awake for what seemed like long hours, I heard nothing more.

Maybe it was, like Cap suggested, a trick of the wind. But I didn't believe it.

CHAPTER 8

NOR WAS IT a trick of the wind. Somewhere in those mountains I knew there was something . . . or somebody. . . .

When daylight came I was high in the hills. There was no trail where I rode. To the south there was, but I had switched off. I rode up into the trees, then got down from my horse and switched to moccasins. I went back over my tracks and smoothed them out. Then I mounted up again and headed higher.

Pines grew thick, giving way to spruce. Sometimes I was weaving among trees so close there was scarce room to pass, and half the time I was bent down low to get under branches, or was walking on the soft pine needles and leading that appaloosa.

It was in my mind that I would come out on the ridge not far from that first keyhole pass, and it worked out that way. I found myself on a crest where I could see far and away in all directions.

To the north a huge peak called Storm King shouldered against the bright sky, with sunlight on the snow. The canyon of the Vallecitos, through which I'd climbed, fell away steeply below me, and on my right I could look for miles over some of the most rugged country I ever saw.

I rode into the high valley where that ghost lake was. It looked unchanged until I got near it. My old trail was partly covered over by water. There had been rains since my last trip, and the lake was acres larger despite the run-off.

The trail down the chute was about the same. Maybe there was a mite more water over the trail, but not enough to interfere. Riding into my lonely valley, I felt like I was coming home.

First off, I checked the tree where I had left the meat hanging. The meat was gone, but there were no bones about, as there would have been if a wild animal had pulled it down. If there had been any tracks the rain had beat them out.

Next I went on to the mine, and scouted around. I left everything as it was, only I staked a claim, marking down its limits on a piece of tanned hide so's I'd have a map if it came to trouble.

Then I set out to scout that valley, for it was in my mind that there must be an easier way out. And I discovered that the stream flowing down the chute actually flowed *north*. Then it took a sharp bend to the west and flowed down from the mountain to join the Vallecitos. For the first time I realized that the stream beside which Cap and I had camped was not the one that fell down the chute.

A dim trail, maybe left by ancient Indians, headed off to the east, and far off I could see several other high lakes. And, riding up through the trees to the ridge top, where I could look the country over, I found that across the valley and beyond a ridge was still another long, high valley. Through it a stream flowed almost due north.

Among the trees that lined the ridges which bordered these valleys there was some grass, but in the valley bottoms there were meadows, rich and green. Remembering the short-grass range country of Texas and the high plains, I thought what magnificent summer range these high valleys would make.

But my concern now was to find a new trail down to the Vallecitos and, if possible, to learn who lived up here and had taken my meat.

Riding north, I looked along the ridge toward the end. The valley seemed to be completely enclosed but, farther on, I discovered that it took a sharp turn, narrowed, and came to an end in a wall of forest.

It was there, under the trees, that I found a fresh footprint.

Dismounting, I followed the faint tracks. Here and there grass was still pressed down, so the trail must have been made while the dew was on it, early that very morning. Suddenly I found a snare. Here there were several footprints, but no blood and no hair, so evidently the snare had caught nothing. Squatting on my heels, I studied it. Cunningly done, it resembled no Indian snare I had seen.

I walked my horse across the high meadow that lay beyond the curtain of trees. The ground was nigh covered by alpine gold-flower, bright yellow, and almighty pretty to look at. And along some of the trickles running down from the melting snow a kind of primrose was growing.

The trees were mostly blue spruce, shading off into aspen and, on the high ridges above timberline, there were a few squat bristle-cone pines, gnarled from their endless war with the wind.

A couple of times I found where whoever it was I

was trailing had stopped to pick some kind of herb out of the grass, or to drink at a stream.

All of a sudden I came to a place where the tracks stopped. Here the person had climbed a big rock, and grass stains had rubbed off the moccasins onto the rock. The meaning was plain enough. He, she, it, or whatever, had caught sight of me trailing it.

From atop the boulder I sighted back down the way I had come and, sure enough, my back trail could be seen at a dozen points in the last few miles.

So I sat down on the rock and took time to study the country. Unless I was mistaken, that party was somewhere not too far off, a-looking me over. What I wished was for them to see I meant no harm.

After a while, I went back to my horse, which had been feeding on the good meadow grass. I rode across a trickle of water and up a long gouge in the mountainside until I topped out where there was nothing but a few bristle-cone pines, a kind of gray gravel, and some scattered, lightning-struck trees.

Off to my right, and some distance ahead, I could see a stream running down the mountain to the northeast. It looked like here was another way out of this jumble of ridges and mountain meadows.

Starting the appaloosa ahead, I saw his ears come up. Following his look, I saw a movement, far off, at the edge of a clump of aspen on a slope. But before I could get out my glasses, whatever it was had gone.

Riding on, I came to a place where somebody had been kneeling beside a snow-stream, evidently for a drink. If my guessing was right that was the third drink in the last couple of hours. Possibly it was less time than that . . . and in this high country, with moisture in the air, it seemed too much drinking. Nor was the weather that warm.

Puzzled, I started on again. All of a sudden the tracks weren't hard to follow. Whoever it was had headed straight for some place, and was too busy getting there to think of covering trail . . . or else I was believed to be lost down below somewhere.

A moment later I saw where the person I followed had fallen down, then got up, and gone on.

Sick . . . that drinking could mean fever.

Sick and, unless I missed my guess, all alone.

The tracks disappeared. It took me several minutes of circling and scouting to find the likely spot. From here on it was judgment more than tracks, for the person had taken to rock, and there was a-plenty of it.

The appaloosa made work of scrambling over that rock, so I got down and walked.

It was coming up to night, and there was no way I knew of to get down off the mountain at night.

Time to time I stopped, trying the air for smoke or sound, but there was none.

Whatever I was hunting had taken off in a wild area of boulders and lightning-struck trees, where the gray ridges had been lashed and whipped by storm.

Off on the horizon I could see great black thunderheads piling up, and I knew this place would be hell during an electrical storm. Somehow I had to get down from there, and fast. Time or two before, I'd been caught in high peaks by a storm, although never so high as this. I'd seen lightning leaping from peak to peak, and sometimes in sheets of blue flame.

The boulders were a maze. Great slabs of rock stood on knife edges, looking like rows of broken molars, split and rotten. Without warning, a canyon dropped away in front of me for maybe five hundred feet of almost sheer fall. Off to the left I could see an eyebrow of trail.

Anywhere off that bald granite ridge would look like heaven to me, and I hurried to the trail. Once I heard rocks fall behind my horse, but we kept going down, with me walking and leading.

When I reached the meadow at the foot of the trail, I looked up. It was like standing on the bottom of a narrow trough with only the dark sky above me.

The trail led out of the meadow, and on it were those same tracks. Hurried by the storm, I followed them.

Thunder rumbled like great bowling balls in an empty hall of rock. Suddenly, an opening appeared in the wall ahead of me and I drew up, calling out.

There was no answer.

Leaving the appaloosa, I shucked my gun. In front of the opening there was a ledge, maybe thirty yards along the face of the cliff, and a dozen yards deep. A body could see folks had lived and worked there for some time. I called out again, and my voice echoed down the canyon.

There was only the fading echo, only the silence, and emptiness. A few large drops of rain fell. I went slowly across to the mouth of the cave.

A sort of wall had been fixed up, closing off part of the opening. It was made of rocks, fitted together without mortar. Stepping around it, I looked inside.

On the wall hung an old bridle. In a corner was a dried-up saddle and a rifle. Dead coals were in a fireplace that had seen much use. Over against the wall was a pallet, and on the pallet a girl was lying.

I struck a match, and got the shock of my life. She was a young girl, a little thing, and she was mighty pretty. A great mass of red-gold hair spilled over the worn blankets and bearskins on which she was lying. She wore a patched-up dress, and moccasins. Her cheeks were flushed red.

I spoke to her, but she made no sound. Bending over, I touched her brow. She was burning up with fever.

And then the storm broke.

It took me only a couple of minutes to rush outside and get my horse. There was an adjoining cave— actually part of the one the girl was in—that had a crude manger. At one time a horse or mule had been kept there.

When I had tied my horse I went back and, taking wood from a stack by the entrance, I kindled a fire and put some water on to heat.

With a fire going I could see better, and I found another blanket to cover her over with. It was plain enough that two folks had been living here, though there was only one now. Likely there had been only one for quite a stretch.

The rifle had been cleaned, but the chamber was empty and there was no ammunition anywhere I looked. There was a flint knife with quite an edge to it—probably the knife used to cut my meat that first time.

Looked to me this girl had been living here quite some time, and by the look of her, not living too well. She was mighty slight, almighty slight.

When that water was boiling I fixed some coffee and, with my own jerked beef, made some broth.

Outside the thunder was rolling something awful and there were lightning flashes almost two or three a minute, seemed like, lighting up that gorge where the cave was. Rain was falling in great sheets, and when the lightning flashed I could see the rocks glistening with it.

Cap was down at our camp by himself, and the country would be filling up with mighty unpleasant folks. I was realizing that after a rain like this nobody could get back up that chute, and unless there was another way out, I was stuck. And me with a sick girl on my hands.

When I had that broth hot, I held the girl in my arms and fed her some of it. She was out of her head, delirious-like. It seemed to me she had got back to the cave with her last strength, but she tasted that broth and liked it.

After a while she went back to sleep.

Back home on the Cumberland we did for ourselves when it came to trouble and sickness, but in a storm like this there was no chance to go out and get any herbs or suchlike. All I could do was keep her from getting chilled and build up her strength with broth.

Might be she only had a cold, and I was praying it wasn't pneumonia or anything like that. She was run down some, and probably hadn't been eating right. What she could get from her snares wouldn't amount to much, and she had no weapons to kill anything larger. What bothered me was how she got into this wild country in the first place.

While she slept I hunted around the cave and found a man's wore-out boots, and a coat hanging on the wall. I taken that down and used it for more cover over her.

Hours later, while the storm was still blowing and lightning jumped peak to peak, crashing like all get-out, she awakened and looked around, and called to somebody whose name I couldn't make out. All I could do was feed her some more of that broth, but she took to it like a baby to mother's milk.

All night long I sat by that fire, keeping it bright in case she awakened and was scared. Toward daylight the storm played itself out and went rumbling away far off down the mountains.

I rigged a line and went down to the creek. The chances of getting fish after the storm didn't look too good, with the water all riled. Nonetheless, I threw out a hook. After a while I hooked a trout and, about a half-hour later, another one.

Up at the cave the red-haired girl was sleeping quietly, so I went to work and cleaned those trout and fried them up. I started some coffee and then went outside.

Wandering around, I came on a grave. Actually, I could see it wasn't a dug grave, but a wide crack in the rock. Rocks had been rolled in at each end and the cracks tamped in with some kind of clay which had settled hard. Over the grave was scratched a name and a date.

JUAN MORALES
1790–1874

He had died last year, then.

And that meant this girl had been here in this canyon all alone for almost a year. No wonder she was run down.

Juan Morales had been eighty-four years old when he died. Too old a man to be traipsing around the mountains with a young girl. From his name he had been a Spanish man, but she did not look like any Spanish girl I'd ever seen. Yet I'd heard it said that some of them were blonde, so maybe they were red-headed, too.

I went back to the cave and looked at my patient. She was lying there looking at me, and the first thing she said was, "Thank you for the venison."

She had the bluest eyes.

"Ma'am," I said, "I'm William Tell Sackett, Tell for short, and leaving the meat was little enough to do."

"I'm Ange Kerry," she said, "and I'm most glad you found me."

Only thing I couldn't figure out was how a girl that pretty ever got lost.

CHAPTER 9

ANGE HAD GONE to sleep again so, after adding sticks to the fire, I went out and sat down in the mouth of the cave. It was the first good chance I'd had to look around me.

The valley where I found the gold was lonely but peaceful ... this was wild. Sheer black cliffs surrounded it on nearly all sides, broken here and there as though cracked by some thunderous upheaval of the mountain. The foot of each crack ended in a slope of talus, with broken, barkless tree trunks, their branches thrown wide and white against the rock like skeleton arms.

The stream descended through the valley in a series of ripples and miniature cascades, gathering here and there in a pool, only to go tumbling off down into the wild gorge that seemed to end in space.

The trees that rimmed the canyon were dwarfed and twisted, leaning away from prevailing winds, trees that the years gave no stature, only girth and a more tenacious grip on the rock from which they grew.

Landslides had carried away stands of aspen and dumped them among the tumbled boulders along the bottom. Slabs and crags of rock had broken off from the cliff faces and lay cracked and riven upon the canyon floor. There was scarcely a stretch of level land anywhere, only here and there an arctic meadow or stretch of tundra. The rocks were colored with lichen—green, orange, reddish, black, or gray—crusting the rocks, forever working at them to create from their granite flanks the soil that would build other growth.

The matlike jungles of arctic willow hedged the stream in places, and streaks of snow and ice lay along cracks where the sun could not reach.

About an hour short of noon the sun came over the mountain and warmed the cave mouth. New streams melted from the snow banks, and I watched several mountain sheep go down a narrow thread of trail. A big old black bear showed on the mountain opposite. Had I shot him it would have taken me all day to get where he was. Anyway, he wasn't bothering me.

Despite the quiet of the place, there was something wild and terrible about it that wouldn't let me settle down. Besides that, I couldn't keep from worrying about Cap.

It was midafternoon when Ange Kerry woke up again, and I went back in and fixed her a cup of coffee.

She looked up at me. "You've no idea how good that tastes. I've had no coffee for a year."

"Thing puzzles me," I said, "is why you came up here in the first place. You came with that Juan Morales?"

"He was my grandfather. He and my grandmother raised me, and when she died he began to worry about dying and leaving me with nothing. Grandfather had an old map that had been in our family for years, telling of gold in the San Juans, so he decided to find it for me. I insisted on coming with him.

"He was very strong, Tell. It seemed nothing was too much for him. But we couldn't follow the map, and we got lost in the mountains. We were short of ammunition. Some of it we lost in a rock slide that injured his shoulder.

"We found this place, and he was sure it was close by—the gold, I mean. He never told me why he believed it, but there was some position in relation to two mountain peaks. One was slightly west of north, the other due west.

"Grandfather must have been hurt worse in the slide than he let me know. He never got better. One of his shoulders was very bad, and he limped after that, and worried about me. He said we must forget the gold and get out as best we could.

"Then he became ill . . . that was when you came into the valley, and when I took some venison from you at night."

"You should have awakened me."

"I—I was afraid."

"Then when you came back and found the venison I left for you . . . you knew I was all right then?"

"I thought—oh, I don't know what I thought! When I came back here after getting that first piece of meat, that was when grandfather died. I told him about you."

"He died then?"

"He told me to go to you, that you would take me out of here, and that most men were good to women."

"When I saw the grave I thought he'd been dead longer than that."

"I wasn't sure of the date. We lost track of time, up here."

She must have had a rough time of it. I thought of that while I went to work and made some more broth, only this time with chunks of meat in it.

"How did you get into this place?"

"We came up a trail from the north—an ancient trail, very steep, or perhaps it was a game trail."

From the north, again. What I wanted was a way down on the west. The way I figured, we couldn't be much more than a mile from Cap right now, but the trouble was that mile was almost straight down.

Ange Kerry was in no shape to leave, and with all the men hunting me that had a figuring to fill me full up with lead, I wasn't planning to go down until I could take Ange along. Suppose I was killed before anybody knew where she was?

Just in case, I told her how things were. "We got us a camp. Cap Rountree and me, down on the Vallecitos, west of here. If something happens to me, you get to him. He'll take you to my folks down to Mora."

Seemed likely that with another few days of rest she might be ready to try coming down off that mountain. Mostly she was starved from eating poorly.

I went out and went across the canyon. There I looked back, taking time to study that cliff. A man might climb that slope of talus and work his way to the top of the cliff through the crack that lay behind it. A man on foot might.

Chances were that right down the other side was camp. Studying it out, I decided to have a try at it.

Down by the stream I had seen an outcropping of talc, so I broke off a piece and scratched out *Back Soon* on a slab of rock.

Taking my rifle, I rigged myself a sling from a rawhide strip, and headed for that slope. Climbing the steep talus slope was work, believe me. That rock slid under my feet and every time I took three steps I lost one, but soon I got up to that crack.

Standing there looking up, I was of a mind to quit, though quitting comes hard to me. That crack was like a three-sided chimney, narrow at the bottom, widening toward the top. The slope above the chimney looked like it was just hanging there waiting for a good reason to fall. Yet by holding to the right side a man might make it.

I hung my rifle over my back to have my hands free, and started up that chimney and made it out on the slope. Holding on to catch my breath, I looked down into the canyon.

It made a man catch his breath. I swear, I had no idea I'd climbed so high up. The creek was a thread, the cave mouth looked no bigger than the end of a fingernail, and I was a good two thousand feet above the floor of the valley. My horse, feeding in the meadow where I'd left him on a picket-rope, looked like an ant.

Clinging to the reasonably solid rock along the side of the rock slide, I worked my way to the top, and was wringing wet by the time I got there.

Nothing but sky and cloud above me, and around me bare, smooth granite, with a hollow where there was snow, but nowhere any trees or vegetation. I walked across the top of that ridge, scoured by wind and storm . . . the air was fresher than a body could believe, and a light wind was blowing.

In a few minutes I was looking down into the valley of the Vallecitos.

A little way down the forest began, first scattered, stunted trees, then thick stands of timber. Our camp—I could see a thin trail of smoke rising—was down there among them.

From where I stood to the point where camp was, I figured it to be a half-mile, if it was level ground. But the mountain itself was over a mile high, which made the actual distance much greater. Here and there were sheer drops. And there would be no going straight down. One cliff I could see would take a man almost a mile north before he could find a place to get down.

Off where Cap and me had laid out the town site there was a stir of activity. There were several columns of smoke, and it looked like some building going on, but it was too far to make out, even in that clear air.

It was sundown when I got back to the cave, and Ange broke into a smile when I showed up.

"Worried?"

She smiled at me. "No . . . you said you'd come back."

She was looking better already. There was color in her cheeks and she had started to make coffee. Coming back I had killed a bighorn sheep, and we roasted it over the fire, and had us a grand feast. That night we sat talking until the moon came up.

After she went to sleep I sat in the door of the cave and watched the moon chin itself on the mountains, and slowly slide out of sight behind a dark fringe of trees.

At dawn, five days later, we pulled out.

We crossed toward that stream that ran down to the north or northeast and followed the old game trail Ange had mentioned. She showed me where they had lost their pack mule with some of their grub, and then she told me that there was a way which would lead down to our camp, a deer and sheep trail off to the south of the canyon.

With Ange riding and me leading the appaloosa among those rocks and thick forests, it was slow going and it took a long time to get to the bottom. I led the horse on through the trees until I reached a point maybe a half-mile from the town site.

There must have been forty men working around over there, with buildings going up, but I could see no sign of Cap. Somehow the set-up didn't look right to me.

I helped Ange down from the horse. "We'll rest," I said. "Come dark, we'll go to our camp. That bunch over there look like trouble." I'd no idea of facing up to a difficulty with a sick girl on my hands.

Dark came on slowly. Finally, thinking of Cap, it wasn't in me to wait longer. I helped Ange back into the saddle, and took my Winchester from the scabbard.

It was a short walk across a meadow and into the willows. Nothing stirred except the nighthawks which dipped and swung in the air above us. Somewhere a wolf howled. The sun was down, but it was not yet dark.

We turned south. Wearing my moccasins, I made

little sound in the grass, and the appaloosa not much more. There was a smell of smoke in the air, and a gentle drift of wind off the high peaks.

All I could think of was Cap Rountree. If that crowd at the town site were the wrong bunch—and I had a feeling they were—then Cap was bad hurt or killed. And if he was killed I was going up to that town and read them from the Book. I was going to give that bunch gospel.

The first of the three men who came out of the brush ahead of me was Kitch.

"We been waiting for you, Sackett," he said, and he lifted his gun. He thought sure enough he had me.

Trouble was, he hadn't seen that Winchester alongside my leg. I just tilted it with my right hand, grabbed the barrel with my left, and shot from the hip. While he was swinging that gun up, nonchalant and easy, I shot him through the belly. Without moving from my tracks I fired at the second man, and saw him go spinning.

The third one stood there, white-faced and big-eyed, and I told him, "Mister, you unloose that gun belt. If you want to, you just grab that pistol . . . I'm hoping you do."

He dropped his gun belt and backed off a step.

"Now we're going to talk," I said. "What's your name?"

"Ab Warren . . . I didn't mean no harm." He hesitated. "Mister, Kitch ain't dead . . . can I do for him?"

"He'll get another bullet 'less he lies still," I replied. "You want to help him, you talk. Where's my partner?"

The man shifted his feet. "You better hightail it. The others'll be down here to see."

"Let 'em come. You going to talk?"

"No, I ain't. By—"

By that time I'd moved in close and I backhanded him across the mouth. It was a fairly careless blow but, like I said, my hands are big and I've worked hard all my life.

He went down, and I reached over and took him by the front of his shirt and lifted him upright.

"You talk or I'll take you apart. I'll jump down your throat and jollop your guts out."

"They ambushed him, but he ain't dead. That ol' coon Injuned away in the brush and downed two before they pulled off. He's back at your camp, but I don't think he's doing so good."

"Is he alone?"

"No . . . Joe Rugger's there with him." Warren paused. "Rugger took up for him."

Kitch was moaning. I walked over to him. "I didn't run, did I, Kitch?" I turned on Warren. "If he lives, and I ever see him carrying a gun, here, in Texas or Nebraska, I'm going to kill him on sight. That goes for you, too. If you want to stay around, stay. But if you wear a gun, I'll kill you."

Taking up the bridle, I added, "You go back up there and tell that outfit that all those who didn't make a deal with Cap for their lots can move, or be moved by me. We staked and claimed that town site and we cut tumber for the buildings."

"There's forty men up there!" Warren said.

"And there's one of me. But you tell them. I hope

they are gone before I have to come read them from the Book."

Scooping up his guns and the others, I started off.

It was full dark by the time we got to the camp, and I heard a challenge. The voice sounded familiar, but it wasn't Cap.

"Sackett here," I said, "and I got a lady for company. I'm coming in."

Falling back beside her, I said, "Ma'am, I'm sure sorry about back yonder. Folks never reckoned me a quarrelsome man, but I'd trouble with these men before."

She did not reply and suddenly scared, I said, "Look—you ain't hurt, are you?"

"No . . . I'm not hurt."

Her voice sounded different, somehow, but I didn't think much of it until I reached up and helped her down. She felt stiff in my hands, and she wouldn't look at me.

A man stepped up beside us. "Sackett? I'm Joe Rugger. Remember? I spoke of coming back to see you. I've been trying to keep them off Cap."

Rugger was the square-set man who had ridden with Kitch. Brushing past him, I went to the lean-to. Cap was lying there on his blankets, and he was so pale it scared me.

"Most times we haven't dared have a light," Rugger said. "They've been pot-shooting around here at night."

"Put the light out."

For a few minutes I sat there, scared to death. That old man looked bad off, mighty bad off. We hadn't been together long, but I'd come to be fond of him. He was a solid, true-blue old man.

"They ambushed him . . . four, five of them. They shot him out of his saddle and then went hunting him like an animal. Only Cap was clear conscious and he let them come in close where he couldn't miss. He killed two and the rest took off like scared polecats."

"Where's he hit?"

"Missed the lung, I think. Took him high, but he lost a lot of blood before he got here. I didn't know of it until the next morning. Then I came right up.

"When they came to finish him off, I stopped them before they could get to the trees. Cap, he came out of it and managed to get off a shot . . . they think he's in better shape than he is."

I walked outside and stood under the trees. If that old man died I'd hunt every man jack of them down and gut-shoot them.

By now they had seen Kitch and they knew I was back. If I knew that crowd over there, tonight they would argue, they would threaten, and they would make wartalk, but unless I was completely wrong, they wouldn't come down here in the dark. Not after what happened to Kitch. Tomorrow I could expect trouble.

However I would be ready, and if they wanted it tonight instead of tomorrow, they could have it.

Last thing I'd wanted was trouble, but they'd called the turn, and now they would get a bellyful of it. If they wanted to start the town with a line of graves in boot hill, it would be that way.

Joe Rugger came up behind me. "You want I should ride south for Orrin and Tyrel?"

"No, sir. No, I don't. This here is myself, and I don't think there's going to be enough of it to go around."

They could have forty-eight hours. Then I was riding down.

CHAPTER 10

MORNING BROKE WITH an overcast sky and a hint of rain, and rain worried me because down here rain could mean snow in the mountains where the gold was.

First off, I walked out to the edge of the timber that surrounded our camp and looked toward the town site. There were several tents, one building already up, and a couple more on the way.

Nobody seemed to be pulling out.

Joe Rugger was squatting over the fire with a long fork, working on some venison steaks. Ange was helping him, but when she looked at me her eyes were bleak and frightened.

Not that I could blame her. It must have come as a shock to come out of the peace of those hills and run into a gunfight . . . and my way of doing things must have been a shock. Folks who live sheltered or quiet lives, away from violent men, have no idea how they have to be dealt with. And I never was one to stand around and talk mean . . . if there's fighting to be done the best thing is have at it and get it over with.

Those men at the town site had had their warning, and I gave them time to think about it. In any such number of men a few of them with nerve will stand up to trouble; they will be tough, resolute men. A few will be talkers willing to ride along with the crowd; a few will be camp-followers ready to pick up the leav-ings of stronger men. And of course, there is always the kind who is himself a tough man, if given leader-ship.

Such a warning as I had given was apt to thin their ranks somewhat. A few of the camp-followers would shy from trouble, and some of the talkers would make an excuse and ride out.

Cap was in bad shape. He had lost a lot of blood, like Rugger said, and he was a thin, tough old man without too much blood in him. He ran mostly to bone and sinew.

It scared me when I looked at him. His cheeks were sunken in and his eyes were hollow. He looked a sight.

"Ange," I said, "will you see what you can do for him?"

"Yes."

"Ange, I'm sorry about last night."

"You didn't have to shoot those men. That was wicked! It was an awful thing!"

"They were mighty bad men. They came out there to kill me, Ange."

"I don't believe it. They were just talking."

"Ange, when men carry guns they don't just talk about killing. When a man mentions killing, and has in his hands or on his person the means to kill, then you have a right to believe he means to do what he says. I've helped bury a few men who tried to argue at times like that."

Ange wasn't doing any trading on that kind of talk. She walked away from me and left me standing, and all that sort of nice feeling between us was gone.

Only girl I ever felt likely to care for, and she would have none of me.

And after I did what I would have to do, she was going to like me even less. But the fact of the matter is, no man can shape his life according to woman's thinking. Nor should any woman try to influence a man toward her way. There must be give and take between them, but when a man faces a man's problems he has to face them a man's way.

We had come up here asking trouble of no one. We had staked a claim, measured out a town site, and staked out building sites. We had cut timber and prepared to build; and then strangers came in, jumped our town site, and tried to jump our claim. They had shot Cap, and they had tried to kill me.

Nobody talked much over breakfast. After breakfast I taken Blackstone and sat down under a tree where I could watch that town site, and I read. Reading was not easy for me, but I hooked both spurs in the girth and settled down for a long ride, determined not to let it throw me. When words showed up that wore an unfamiliar brand, I passed them by and went on, but usually they made sense to me after some study.

After an hour I toted my book back to camp and, rounding up a pick and shovel, headed for the creek.

Cap had sunk a shaft to bedrock and started a cleanup. Going down into the shaft I widened it out a mite and got out some gravel. At the edge of the stream I went to work with the pan, filling it with gravel, dipping it into the water, and starting the water swirling to wash the sand over the edge. I found color, but not much.

Several times I walked to the edge of the woods. Noon came and I could see no sign of work around the town, so evidently they were drinking and talking. Cap was breathing easier, and Ange was feeding him when I came into camp, but she paid me no mind and I sat down to eat what there was.

If they made an all-out attack on us, we might be able to hold them off, but if we had to get out of there our only chance was up the mountain, and with a sick man on our hands we weren't likely to get far.

Taking an axe, I went out to check our defenses. I added a few logs, and rooted out some brush here and there to give us a better field of fire.

Joe Rugger was worried, I could see that, but there was no rabbit in him. He had come in with us and he planned to stick.

"What led you to throw in with us, Joe?" I asked him.

"Drifted in here with the wrong crowd before I measured them for calibre. Seemed to me you and Rountree were more my type. Fact was, I figured to try leasing that store from you. Back in Ohio I operated a small store for another man, but it seemed to me I'd get nowhere working for the other fellow, so I quit. I've done some mining, but a store is what I always wanted."

"Joe, you've just bought yourself a lease. Cap and me, we want to build a town that shapes up to something, and we would be proud to lease that store to you."

"Thanks, Tell."

It made a body restless, wondering what they were cooking up down there in town. Same time, I never was one to keep a serious view of things. Time to time folks get the idea I'm slighting my problems because ofttimes they strike me as funny. Now I kept thinking of all those men down there, arguing and drinking and drinking and arguing, and working up a nerve to come after us. It struck me, a man might sort of wander down there of a nighttime and have himself some fun.

Rousting around in our gear I found about a hundred feet of rope Cap had packed along, on account of rope is always handy. Joe had some more, and I knotted the two together and went inside and got my field glasses and studied that town.

There were four tents—one large, like the saloon tents at the end of the tracks in railroad towns, and the others small. A couple of horses were saddled, with packs behind the saddles . . . some men were in the street.

Something about it bothered me. If there actually were forty men around the town, where were they?

I took my Winchester and scouted around the edge of the trees, studying the bench, searching every possible approach. It scarcely seemed likely that they would try another attack with me here, when Cap and Joe had driven them off alone. But they might.

Thinking of it worried me, with Ange Kerry at the camp, and Cap Rountree a sick man. Looked to me like I was going to have to go after them, after all.

Come evening time, Joe Rugger came out to stand watch, and I went into camp for grub. Cap was conscious and he looked up at me. "You've got it all on your hands, Tell. I'll be no help to you."

"You've been a help." I squatted on my heels

beside his pallet, nursing a cup of coffee in my hands. "Cap, I'm going to take it to them tonight."

"You be careful."

"Else they'll come a-hunting. We can't have them shooting around with Ange here, and you laid up."

"That's a fine girl."

"You should see that country up yonder. Blessed if I can see how she made it . . . months up there, all alone."

I could see Cap was done up. He would need time and plenty of good food to get his strength back . . . it was lucky Ange was there.

She came in, bringing a cup of soup for Cap, but she kept her eyes away from me. What did she expect me to do? Stand still and get shot? Sure, I got the jump, but Kitch had warning. And when he came out of the trees like that he wasn't looking to play patty-cake.

She was mighty pretty. A little thing, slim and lovely. Though the only clothes she had were wore-out things, and she was not likely to have better until one of us could cut loose for Silverton or Del Norte.

Her face had taken on some color, and she had combed out that hair of hers and done it up like some of those fancy pictures I'd seen in *Godey's Lady's Book*. I declare, she was pretty!

"See you," I said, and stood up. "You take care."

There was a moment there I thought of talking with her, but what could I say? Seemed to me she didn't want any words from me, and I went away feeling mighty miserable inside. Walking out to the edge of the trees, I stood looking toward the two or three lights and thinking what a fool a man could be.

What was she, after all? Just a slim girl with a lot of red-gold hair . . . nothing to get upset about.

The humor of what I'd been thinking of doing there in town went out of me. I looked at that town and felt like walking over there and shooting it out.

Only there was no sure way I could win if I did that, and I had to win. Joe was a solid man, but he was no gunfighter. First time in my life I wished I could look up and see Tyrel coming down the pike.

Only Tyrel was miles away and days away, and whatever happened now was up to me. Anyway, it never does a man much good to be thinking of what he could do if he had help . . . better spend his time figuring a way of doing it himself.

Gathering up that rope, I taken it to my horse and saddled up.

"Joe," I said, "you be careful. They may come a-winging it over this way. If they do, and if I'm able, I'll come a-smoking, but you stand 'em off until I get here."

Ange was standing with the fire behind her and I couldn't see her face. Only when I rode out, I lifted a hand. "See you," I said, and let the palouse soft-foot if off the bench and into the streambed.

It was cool, with no wind. The clouds were low, making it especial dark. There was a smell of pine woods in the air, and a smell of wood smoke and of cooking, too.

Nigh the town site I drew up and got down, tying the appaloosa to some willows in the streambed. I put my hand on his shoulder. "Now you stand steady, boy. I won't be gone long."

But I wondered if that was truth or not.

Maybe it would be just as well if I was to get the worst of them. That Ange, now—she had no use for me, and sure as shooting I was getting a case on her.

Not that it was likely she could ever see me. Girl that pretty had her choice of men. Nobody ever said much about me being good-looking—except Ma— and even Ma, with the best intentions in the world, looked kind of doubtful when she said it.

I didn't shape up to much except for size. Only thing I could do better than anybody else I knew was read sign . . . and maybe shoot as good as most. Otherwise, all I had was a strong back.

That Blackstone, now. I'd been worrying that book like a dog worries a bone, trying to get at the marrow of it, but it was a thing took time. Days now I'd been at it, off and on, and everything took a sight of thinking out.

He said a lot of things that made a man study, although at the windup they made a lot of sense. If I could learn to read . . . I would never get to be a lawyer like Orrin there, but . . .

This was no time for dreaming. Pa, he always advised taking time for contemplating, but this was the wrong time.

Taking that rope and my Winchester, I edged in close. Working soft on moccasin feet, I ran my rope through the guy ropes of that big tent, up behind about four guy ropes, and then a loop clean around one of the smaller tents and around the guy ropes of another. Then I walked back to my horse and loosed him, mounting up and taking a dally around the pommel with the loose end.

Everything at the town seemed mighty peaceful.

Inside I could hear folks a-cutting up some touches, the clatter of glasses and poker chips. Seemed almost a shame to worry them.

Walking my horse alongside the building, I stood up on the saddle and pulled myself to the roof. I slid out of my shirt, and shoved it into the chimney. Then I stepped back to the eaves and, about time I touched saddle, all hell broke loose inside. The room had started to fill up with wood smoke and I heard folks a-swearing something awful and coughing.

Turning my horse, I taken a good hold on that rope, let out a wild Comanche yell, and slapped spurs to that palouse.

Those spurs surprised him. He taken out like a scared rabbit. Ripping down those guy ropes and collapsing the other tents, I lit out. When I'd done what I could that way, I rode back through between the tents at a dead run. As I came through, a gang of men rushed up and caught themselves in a loop of rope.

It tumbled the lot of them, and dragged some. I let go the rope and, leaning from the saddle, I wrenched loose a length of tent stake. I rode up on that bunch and rapped a skull here and there.

A man on the stoop of the store building grabbed his pistol. I tossed that stake at his face and said, "Catch!"

He jumped back, fell over the last step and half inside the door.

Riding by, I drew up in the shadow. I'd sure enough played hob. Two small tents had collapsed and folks were struggling under them. The big tent was leaning away over. There was a lot of shouting, and somebody yelled, "No, you don't! Drop that money!" A shot was fired.

I remembered Pa's advice then, and taken time to contemplate. Setting my horse there in the shadows, I watched that mess-up and enjoyed it.

There was swelling under those tents, everybody arguing and swearing. Nobody was making any kind of sense.

One tent flattened down as the men struggled from under it. I decided they needed light, so I taken a flaming stick from the outside fire and tossed it at that flattened-out tent.

Somebody saw me and yelled. I turned sharp and trotted my horse away just as he let go with a shotgun. Then that tent burst into flame and I had to move back further.

They wanted to settle on my town site without paying, did they? They wanted to shoot up my camp?

I happened to notice their corral on the edge of the wash. A couple of saddles, a rope . . . Shaking out a loop, I caught a corner post of the corral with my rope and rode off, pulling it down. Horses streamed by me.

Surely does beat all what a man can do when he sets his mind to being destructive.

One leg hooked around my saddlehorn, I spoke gentle to my horse to warn him of trouble to come, and then I turned my head to the sky.

"*When I walked out on the streets of Laredo, when I—*"

A bullet cut wind near me, and I taken off. Seemed like nobody liked my singing.

CHAPTER 11

THERE WAS A faint lemon color edging the gray of the clouds when I rolled out of my blankets. Joe Rugger had teased the fire into flame and put water on for coffee. Sticking my feet into my boots, I stomped them into place and slung my gun belt around my hips. Expecting trouble, that was all I had taken off, except for my vest.

I put on my vest and tucked another gun behind my belt and then walked out to the edge of the woods. Oh, sure, I had my hat on—first thing a cowboy does when he crawls out of bed in the morning is to put his hat on.

Looked to me like somebody was leaving over yonder.

Ange was up, her hair combed as pretty as might be, and sunlight catching the gold of it through a rift in the clouds. She brought me a cup of coffee.

"I suppose you're satisfied with what you've done," she said.

"Thank you, ma'am. . . . Satisfied? Well, now. Takes a lot to satisfy a man, takes a lot to please him if he's any account. But what I did, I did well . . . yes, ma'am, I'm pleased."

"I thought you were a good man."

"Glad to hear you say so. It's an appearance I favor. Not that I've ever been sure what it was made a good man. Mostly I'd say a good man is one you can rely on, one who does his job and stands by what he believes."

"Do you believe in killing people?"

"No, ma'am, not as a practice. Trouble is, if a body gets trouble out here he can't call the sheriff . . . there isn't any sheriff. He can't have his case judged by the law, because there aren't any judges. He can't appeal to anybody or anything except his own sense of what's just and right.

"There's folks around believe they can do anything they're big enough to do, no matter how it tromples on other folks' rights. That I don't favor.

"Some people you can arbitrate with . . . you can reason a thing out and settle it fair and square. There's others will understand nothing but force.

"Joe Rugger now, there's a good man. Cap Rountree is another. They are trying to build something. Those others, they figure to profit by what other people do, and I don't aim to stand by in silence."

"You have no authority for such actions."

"Yes, ma'am, I do. The ideas I have are principles that men have had for many a year. I've been reading about that. When a man enters into society—that's living with other folks—he agrees to abide by the rules of that society, and when he crosses those rules he becomes liable to judgment, and if he continues to cross them, then he becomes an outlaw.

"In wild country like this a man has no appeal but to that consideration, and when he fights against force and brutality, he must use the weapons he has.

"Take Joe Rugger now. He rode in here with a lot

of mighty mean, shiftless folks. He broke with them and came over to us when we were shorthanded. He knew when he made that choice that it might be the death of him.

"Ma'am, I'm not an educated man, but I'm trying to make up for it. Thing is, when folks started to live together, a long time ago, they worked out certain laws, like respecting the rights of others, giving folks the benefit of the doubt, sharing the work of the community . . . that sort of thing.

"Cap and me figured to start a town, and we wanted it to be a good town where there would someday be womenfolks walking the streets to stores and where youngsters could play. And you know something? We've got our first citizen. We've got Joe Rugger."

"I never thought of it that way." She said it grudgingly, and she riled me.

"No, ma'am, folks don't," I said with considerable heat. "People who live in comfortable, settled towns with law-abiding citizens and a government to protect them, they never think of the men who came first, the ones who went through hell to build something.

"I tell you, ma'am, when my time comes to ride out, I want to see a school over there with a bell in the tower, and a church, and I want to see families dressed up of a Sunday, and a flag flying over there. And if I have to do it with a pistol, I'll do it!"

This time I riled her. She walked away stiff-like, and I could see that I'd said the wrong thing.

When I finished my coffee Joe came out to stand guard, and I went back and ate some venison and some sourdough bread dipped in sorghum molasses.

Cap looked a sight better. His eyes were brighter, and there was color in his faded cheeks.

"Well, Cap," I said, "I never had any doubt. You're too mean and ornery to die like this. Way I figure, you'll die in a corner just snapping and grabbing and cutting around you. You'll die with your teeth in somebody if I know you right.

"Now you hurry up and get out of there. Joe and me are getting almighty tired of you laying up while we do all the work."

"How're things?"

"Sober. Looks to me like those folks have started to settle down to think things out. Time I went over and had a talk with them. Time to make a little medicine."

"You be careful."

"I'm a careful man. Time comes to run, I ain't afraid to run. When I ride down there this morning, I'm going for a showdown."

"Wish I could go along."

"You set tight . . . I think they'll stand for reasoning now. I plan to get them to sit down and contemplate. And if they can't cut the mustard that way, they'll get their walking papers."

"All of them?"

"Shucks, there ain't no more than forty."

With my Winchester across my saddle, I rode down. They saw me coming, but I was walking my horse in plain sight and they waited for me. With the exception of that fat man who had come with Kitch to our camp, I saw nobody I knew until Ab Warren came outside. He was not wearing a gun.

"You men have moved into a town site staked and

claimed by Cap Rountree and myself. You took it on yourselves to occupy building sites we had laid out. You taken our timber. Last night you found out a little of what trouble can be. Now I've come down here to arbitrate this matter, and I'm going to do it right here in my saddle.

"When Cap and me moved in here, we had an election. He became mayor and I became town marshal by popular acclamation. It was popular with both of us.

"As Cap is laid up, I'm acting mayor as well as marshal. I am also the town council and the vigilante committee, and any time during these proceedings that anybody wants to challenge my authority, he can have at it.

"We're going to have a town here. I think it's going to be a rich town; but rich or poor, it's going to be law-abiding. Any who aren't ready to stand for that had better saddle up, because until we get some constituted authority (I wasn't real sure what "constituted" meant but it sounded mighty good) I am going to run it with a six-shooter.

"Whoever has occupied that building will move out, starting now. That is to be the general store, and Joe Rugger has a lease on it."

The fat man spoke up. "I'm in that building, and I had it built."

"Who paid for the lumber?"

He hesitated, then blustered. "That's no matter. We found it here and we—"

"It belongs to Cap and me. We valued it at one thousand dollars. Pay for it here and now, or get out of the building. As for the work involved, you can charge that up to poor judgment on your part, and know better next time."

"You can't get away with that!"

"You've got ten minutes to start moving. After that I throw things out—you included."

Ignoring him, I looked the others over. They were a bunch of toughs for the most part, although here and there were some men that looked likely.

"We're going to need a saloon—a straight one. And we're going to need a hotel and an eating house. If any of you want to have a try at it, you'll get cooperation from us."

The fat man was the leader, I could see that, but he was red-faced and mad, not sure of how much backing he would get. Several had pulled out already. Kitch and his partner were dead. Ab Warren was here to tell them how that happened.

Suddenly a burly, unshaved man stepped out of the crowd. "I cooked for a railroad construction crew one time. I'd like to handle that eating house."

"All right, you trim that beard and wash your shirt, and you've got thirty days to prove you can cook grub fit to eat. If you can't, you get somebody who can."

A slim young fellow who looked pale around the gills, like he hadn't been west long, spoke up. "I'm a hotel man, and I can also run a saloon. I can run it honest."

"All right." With my left hand I took a paper from my shirtfront. "Here's the plan Cap and me laid out. You two study that and choose your sites. When you get your plans made, you draw straws to see who builds first; the other helps, and turn about."

It was time to settle things with that fat man. Somebody was speaking low to him and I heard the fat man called Murchison.

"Murchison," I said, "you have about three minutes to get started. And this time I don't mean cleaning out that building. I mean down the road."

"Now, look here—"

My horse walked right up to him. "You came in here to ride roughshod over what you thought was a helpless old man. You showed no respect for the rights of others or the rights of property. You'd be no help to a town. Get on your horse and start traveling."

Pushing my horse forward another step, I backed Murchison up. The appaloosa stepped right up on the stoop after him.

"I'll be back," Murchison said angrily. "The Bigelows are in Silverton."

"We'll hold a place for you," I said, "right alongside of Kitch."

Ab Warren stayed.

Murchison rode from town that morning and about fifteen men rode with him.

There was a Texas Ranger one time who said that there's no stopping a man who knows he's in the right and keeps a-coming. Well, I've often been wrong, but this time I was right and they had to pay mind to me or bury me, and mine is a breed that dies hard.

In the days that followed, other folks began to drift in. The second week a rider came, and then two wagons. Claims were taken up along the creek and one man drove in about thirty head of sheep which he started feeding along the moutainside. Joe Rugger got his store going, Allison his hotel, which he started in the big gambling tent that had been abandoned. Briggs ran a good eating house. Nothing fancy, but simple food, mighty well-cooked. Aside from beef and beans, he served up bear meat, venison, and elk.

We saw nothing of the Bigelows, but we heard aplenty. Tom and Ira were the two we heard most about. They were suspected of holding up a stage near Silverton. Tom had killed a man in Denver City, and had been in a shooting in Leadville. Ira was a gambler, dividing his time between Silverton and some other boom camps.

They had made their brags about me. They would take care of me when they found time. I'd as soon they never found it.

Twice I made trips into the mountains and came back down with gold . . . two muleloads the last time.

Esteban Mendoza and Tina came over and built a cabin in town, near the foot of the mountain, and Esteban had two freight wagons working along the Silverton road.

Ange Kerry moved away from our camp and got a little place in town where she lived, and she worked with Joe Rugger in the store, which combined with the post office and Wells Fargo express. She had never been the same toward me since I killed Kitch and his partner.

She was prettier than ever, and mighty popular around town. Nearly everybody sort of protected her. Joe Rugger brought his wife out and they built a home on the back end of the store.

Cap took a long time mending, and he hadn't

much energy when he was able to walk, so it was up to me to do what was done.

Of an evening I read what newspapers I could find, and kept hammering away at Blackstone. Time to time somebody would drift into camp, stay a while, and drift out again, leaving books behind. I read whatever there was. But mostly I worked.

I built us a three-room log house high on the bench, with my old trail up the mountain right behind it, and the spring close by. I built a strong stable and corral against the coming winter, and I cut a few tons of hay in the meadow.

There was snow on some of the peaks now where I hadn't seen it before. A time or two, early in the morning, there was front in the bottom, and once ice slicked over a bucket of left-out water.

The old barricades I let lie, and I kept the brush trimmed off the mesa. Grass was growing high out there, and there was good grazing for our stock.

When I went to town now there were few whom I knew. Joe Rugger was acting mayor, Allison and Briggs were loyal men. Murchison had come back and started a small gambling house. There were at least two hundred people in town, and she was running like a top.

The aspen began to turn yellow . . . seemed like I'd been here years, though it was only a few months.

There was little trouble. Two men killed each other over a poker game in Murchison's joint, and there was a cutting down on the creek, some private affair over a woman.

One night Cap came in and sat down. "You stay at the books," he said, "and you'll ruin your eyes."

"I've got to learn, Cap."

"You take after those brothers of yours. As soon as they learned to read there was no holding them."

"They've done well."

"Yes, they have. Married, too."

I didn't answer right away, but finally I said, "Well, it takes two."

"You seen Ange lately?"

"You know I haven't."

"That's a mighty fine girl. She won't be around always. I hear that Ira Bigelow is paying her mind."

"Bigelow? Is he in town?"

"Rode in a few days ago while you were in the mountains. Only stayed a few hours, but he managed to meet Ange, and he talked it up to her. He's a handsome man."

Didn't cut much ice, reading about ethics and all. Inside, I could feel myself getting mean. The thought of any of those Bigelows around Ange . . . well, sir, a thing like that could make me mean as an old bear.

Of an evening I would walk outside and look toward the town lights, but I didn't often go down to the street. And it was time for me to make my last trip of the season into the high peaks. I wanted one more load out of there before snow fell. Not that there hadn't been snow up that high, but I had a hunch there was time for one trip. With the new route in, and no need to go by way of the chute, I might make it in and back.

"Going up the mine tomorrow," I told Cap. I stood there a moment. "You know, Ange should come in for a share of that. Her grandpa was hunting it when he died up there . . . he had him a map, and one of those dead Spanish men must have been a relative of his . . . or one of the live ones."

"I was thinking that. Wondered if you'd get around to it."

Picking up my hat, I said, "I think I'll go talk to her."

"You do that," Cap said. "You surely do it."

Anyway, it was time I bought me an outfit—new clothes, and the like. I had money now.

Turning to leave, I stopped. Esteban Mendoza was in the doorway. "Señor Tell? I must speak with you."

He came on into the room. "I was working at my freight wagons fixing some harness, and it became very dark while I sat there, and when I am through I put out the lantern and then sit for a while, enjoying the coolness.

"Beyond the wagon are several men, and they are talking. They do not know I am there, and so I keep very still, for one of them speaks of you. He says you have gold that is not placer gold, but from quartz, from a lode. They believe the mine is in the mountains."

"Who were the men?"

"One is named Tuthill . . . they call him Meester. Another is called Boyd."

Cap looked over at me. "The banker and that gambler from Las Vegas."

"How about the others?"

He shrugged. "I do not know. But I think they plan to follow you into the mountains if you go again."

"Thanks, 'Steban. Thanks very much."

After he left I gave it some thought. It was important to make one more trip up there. I not only wanted to get enough gold to start buying my ranch, but I wanted to cover up the work I'd done at the mine in case somebody found the way up to the valley. The trip was a risk I would have to take.

Cap was getting around pretty good now, better than before, and Esteban would look in on him from time to time. He was well enough to care for himself, and he had friends in the town.

"You going down to see Ange?" Cap asked suddenly. "It's getting late."

I got into my saddle and started for town. The lights seemed brighter than before, and there was excitement in me.

Ange. . . .

A shadow stirred in the brush and I waited a moment before riding on. It was a man all right, and he was watching our camp.

Esteban had been right.

CHAPTER 12

LATE AS IT was, the store was crowded. Joe waved a hand to me from where he stood waiting on a customer, and I glanced toward the other counter where Ange was. If she had noticed me, she gave no sign of it.

Most of the people in the store seemed like newcomers, although there were a couple of familiar faces.

"Mr. Sackett, I believe?"

Turning around, I faced Tuthill. He was a handsome man, no question of it, tall and well-dressed in storebought clothes.

"How are you?" I asked. "I wasn't expecting to see you this far from home. What happened to the bank?"

"I left it in good hands."

Glancing toward Ange, I saw she was no longer busy, so I excused myself and walked over to her. "Ange," I said, "I want to buy some clothes."

Her eyes met mine for the merest instant. "All right."

So I gave her my order, aware that Tuthill was watching from a short distance away. She brought me some shirts, jeans, socks, and a sheepskin coat.

". . . And two boxes of .44's," I said.

Her eyes lifted to mine and her face stiffened.

Abruptly, she turned and walked to the ammunition shelf and took down two boxes and came back, placing them on the counter before me.

"Ange," I said, "I've got to talk to you."

"You brought me out of the mountains and I'm very grateful," she said, "but I don't think—"

"Ange, part of that gold belongs to you. Your grandpa was hunting it, and it was probably some ancestor of his who found it first. So you should have a share."

"Whatever you think is right. There's no need for talk."

She turned away from me with my money and made change.

"Ange," I said, "I had to shoot those men."

"Did you? It was the most brutal, the most callous thing I ever saw! And I thought you were so gentle, so nice—"

She broke off and walked away from me. A moment I stood there. When I turned around, Tuthill was beside me. "I didn't know you knew Ange Kerry," he said.

"You make a habit of listening in when folks are talking?" I was mad. "Look, Tuthill, I think you're no gentleman. I also think you're a thief, and that you travel with thieves. You keep that Boyd out of my sight—do you hear? If I see him, I'll come looking for you both."

Brushing past him, I started for the door. Rugger was there. "Something wrong, Tell?"

Ange was looking at me with something mighty close to horror in her eyes. She could not know about Will Boyd following me down that street in Las

Vegas, or about his connection with Tuthill, or what Esteban had overheard. All she knew was what she heard now—that I had made what looked like an unprovoked attack on an innocent and respectable man.

"Nothing, Joe." My voice lowered. "Only Tuthill's curious about me and that claim of mine. So are the people with him. He followed me here from Las Vegas."

Riding back to the claim, I made up my mind. I would head for the high hills now, before daybreak, get a lead on anybody who might try to follow me, and keep it. Once I came down with the gold, I would head south to Mora or somewhere and buy myself a ranch. Ange could do what she had a mind to.

Every time I came to be near her something happened to make me look worse than I had before. She probably had never seen anyone killed before that night I shot Kitch.

Back at camp, Cap could see I was mad, and he made no comment when I threw a pack together and brought out pack saddles. I was taking two pack-horses, and the appaloosa. There was no need to take much gear . . . I would be gone only two or three days.

Yet, just on chance, I took enough food for a week, and four boxes of .44's, aside from what was in my belt. It was an hour short of day when I mounted up to ride out.

"You be careful," Cap warned.

"I saw Tuthill," I told him. "He smells gold. Through some bank, or Wells Fargo, or something, he's had a smell of that gold . . . and he knows it isn't placer gold."

Holding close against the wall of the mountain, I rode north, weaving among the scattered trees on the bench. It was still overcast and there was a smell of dampness in the air.

Where Rock Creek entered the Vallecitos I turned southeast, riding in the creek bed. By daylight that water would have washed away what tracks I made.

The sun was painting the sky with a lavish brush when I topped out on a rise in the trees and looked back. Far below, several miles back, I saw movement. Sun gleamed for an instant on a rifle barrel.

No use taking a chance on leading them to the mine. So, turning off to my left I went up a rocky ridge, using several switchbacks, and rode over the saddle to the east. About a half-mile off I saw a lake, larger than the one in the high valley. Riding swiftly in that direction, I held to a good pace.

Near the shore of that lake I bedded down for the night, and made camp without a fire.

Awakening to a patter of rain on the leaves overhead, I crawled out on the ground, put on my hat and boots, slung on my gun belt and then rolled my bed.

Without even waiting for coffee, I saddled up and left the woods at a fast trot. Working my way around a dozen small lakes and ponds, I topped out on a ridge overlooking miles upon miles of the most magnificent country under heaven.

Nothing moved through the gray veil of the rain. I rode down into my valley. The mine was as I left it. But the trail along the chute was two feet deep in water, and the rain would soon make it impassable. The other route would have to be my way out.

Picketing my horses, I went into the mine and went to work with my pick. The gold was richer than ever, and the quartz so rotten that it crumbled under my boots.

The rain continued . . . a steady, persistent downfall that could easily turn to snow.

No time to think of Ange . . . nor of Cap, or anything but getting the gold out and down the mountains.

When next I came out the rain had ceased, but there was an odd lightness to the air that left me uneasy, and it bothered the horses also.

Several deer and an elk were feeding in the meadow across the valley, and that might mean a storm was coming. They usually came out about sundown. The valley was quiet, the clouds pressing low down over the peaks. The rain started again, scarcely more than a mist.

Returning to the mine, I worked hard for another hour, and then built a fire and made coffee. My head ached a little from not eating, and it was hard to settle down, with that feeling in the air.

But part of my uneasiness was the fear of being trapped.

Beside my fire I worked long into the night, pounding up the quartz. Maybe the gold I'd come upon was only a pocket. Maybe the quartz would be harder farther down into the rock, or the gold might change its character and require milling to get it out. Of such things I knew next to nothing.

When night came I brought the horses in close to the cave, built a fire deeper inside, and mixed a batch of sourdough bread. I made a good meal before I turned in.

Middle of the night I woke up.

It was cold. I mean, it was really cold. It was colder than I'd ever believed it could be. The horses were crowded together, heads down. I stepped out of the cave into a strange, weird world of ice.

Ice . . . crystal ice in the moonlight that fell through torn clouds. Ice on the trees, ice on the rocks, gleaming ice on the meadow grass. Ice on the willows, making them like a forest of slim glass sticks.

It was strange, and it was beautiful, and it had the shine of death.

Nobody would be traveling any trail in the mountains until that ice was gone. Those eyebrow trails . . . those brink-of-the-precipice trails, those rocky crossings, those sheets of rock—all would be sheets of ice now, where no horse could maintain its footing, where even a man in moccasins would scarcely dare to move.

The thought of the trail into the valley where Ange had been made my hair stand on end.

If the sun came out it would melt fast enough. But it was late in the season . . . suppose it snowed first? Any step might start an avalanche.

Going back inside I built my fire bigger, and then I came out with a piece of sacking and commenced to clean off the horses. Ice was on their winter coats, and it crackled when I broke it free. They knew I was trying to help them and they stood very still, their eyes helpless and frightened.

It was the worst sleet storm I'd ever seen, worse even than the *pogonips* in Nevada. A lot of tree branches had broken under the weight of the ice. It was a white, crystalline world . . . like glass, every-where.

Food . . . I would need food the worst way. With the intense cold I would need more than usual to keep warm, and there was no telling how long I'd be stuck here. Maybe all winter.

There was no sense wasting time. Every step, even on the flat, would be taken at the risk of a broken leg. The trails were out of the question now, the gold itself was unimportant. From now on, it would be a fight to survive.

It was still a couple of hours until daylight, but I got my axe, went outside, and cut a couple of good chunks from a log that I'd dragged up, and built a fire that would last.

The horses stood stiff-legged, afraid to move on the slick ground, so with a shovel I went around and broke up the ice and shoveled some of the waste rock from my mine over the ice.

Then I went to the woods, knocked the ice loose from a tree trunk, cut off the heavier limbs, and packed them back to the cave. The moonlight was gone. I added fuel to my fire, put on the coffeepot, and commenced to study out the situation. There might be some way of getting out that I'd overlooked.

With daylight, the first thing would be to find and kill a deer or two. As long as the cold held I'd not have to worry about the meat spoiling.

Dawn came under a sky of cold gray clouds. I went out and started to hunt for a deer. The appaloosa moved to the edge of the ice that sparkled on the grass and began to paw at it to get at the grass. He was a Montana horse and used to such things.

Shortly before noon I found a buck.

By nightfall it was colder, if anything. I'd butchered my deer and hung the meat up. I'd skinned him properly and saved the hide. If I was here for the winter I was going to need as many such hides as I could get. And all the game I would have a chance at was right there in the valley now.

Huddled in my blankets, I sat over the fire all night long. I was going to have to wall up the mouth of that cave. The wind crept in there, fluttered my fire, and brought the cold with it. The morning broke with the flat gray clouds still shielding the sun, the wind knife-edged and raw, the glassy branches shaking slightly, clashing one against the other like skeleton arms.

The horses tugged woefully at the frozen grass, and the ice cut their lips until they came to me, whimpering. Down by the stream where the grass grew taller, I shattered the ice and cut the grass to take back to them.

This could not go on. Somehow I was going to have to get down the mountain. I wanted to take the horses with me if it could be done. Yet I knew it could not. . . . And without me in this high valley they would die.

That night I broiled a venison steak, and ate it, hunched over the fire, cutting it in strips to handle it better.

Snow fell that night, and when day came one of my packhorses was down with a broken leg. The shot that killed him echoed down the ice-choked valley.

Through lightly falling snow, I went down the valley to the chute. The stream was frozen over, and the chute was a solid mass of ice. The water had risen still more, and the ledge down which the trail wound was now under several feet of water. To get out by that route was out of the question.

Ange had lasted out a winter up here with her grandfather. How had they done it?

Their cave was bigger and better sheltered, and there was a lifetime of firewood in the huge old logs that lay among the boulders . . . but could I get down the trail to the bottom?

Could I even get *to* the canyon? Up where the bristlecone pines grew the wind had a full sweep, and it would be even colder than here. The trail, if I could reach it, was five hundred feet down a sheer face that was probably sheeted in ice.

That would be a last resort. For the time being I would remain where I was and try to last out the storm.

Taking the shovel, I went out and knocked more ice from the grass to give the horses a fighting chance. They knew how to get at it themselves, but the ice roughed up their lips and bloodied their hocks.

The snow kept falling, covering the ice with a thin mantle, making the ice all the more dangerous.

Suddenly the appaloosa's head came up sharply and his ears pricked.

I got out my Winchester. Nothing moved within the limited area I could see through the drifting snow. Listening, I could hear nothing.

Walking with extreme care, I went to the willows

at the edge of the creek and cut several long slender lengths which I carried back to the cave and placed on the floor not too close to the fire.

Always, on the range, I carried with me a bundle of rawhide strips, most of them "piggin strings" for tying the legs of cattle when branding. Every cowhand carried some for emergencies on the range. And I was going to have a use for them now.

The horses showed no tendency to wander, but remained close to the cave. All through the morning and into the afternoon I kept busy reducing the rest of the quartz to gold I could pack out.

When the willow strips were pliable again, I took each of them and bent them into an oval and tied them, selecting the two best ovals to keep. Then with the rawhide strips tied across them, I made rough snowshoes.

Before nightfall I took the rifle, strapped on the snowshoes, and went out to give them a test run. They were not the first pair I had made, and they worked well. Trailing down the valley toward the chute, I saw it was rapidly choking with snow over the ice. Escape by that route was completely out of the question.

I circled around, and ventured toward the valley of Ange's cave. When almost to the bare shoulder where the bristle-cone pines grew, I turned back to reach my cave before dark. It was at that moment that I heard the shot.

Stunned with the shock, I stood stock-still listening to the echo of it racketing against the solemn hills.

The echo lost itself against the snow-clad hillsides and I remained still, shivering a little in the cold, alone in a vast world of sky and snow, scarcely willing to accept what my ears had heard.

A shot . . . here!

It had come from the canyon below. Someone was down there! Someone was at or near Ange's cave.

Here? In this place?

CHAPTER 13

THE SUDDEN CRACK of ice ... the breaking of a tree branch laden with snow? ... No. This had been a shot, clear, sharp, unmistakable.

Tell, I said, *you ain't ... aren't ... alone.*

Who knew of the cave below? Or of the valley? Only Ange, so far as I knew. Cap knew what I'd told him, but Cap couldn't have made it up there even if I'd given exact directions, which I hadn't. He was still too weak.

Ange ... ? That was mighty foolish to consider. She had no reason for coming up.

Whoever had been following me down below? Could they have found some way into that valley? That seemed the most likely.

If I started for the canyon now it would be full dark before I got there, and I'd see nothing anyway. The thing to do would be to go back to the mine and hole up there until daybreak.

One thing was a copper-riveted cinch. If those men were in the canyon they were snowed in like I was, and, unless I was much mistaken, they were a lot less able to cope with it.

We Sacketts had never had much to do with, and back in the mountains we learned to make out on mighty little, but we learned how to rustle. There wasn't one of us boys who hadn't traveled miles by himself and lived off the country before he was six-teen.

Since then I'd had very little but rough time, what with soldiering and all. A Montana-from-Texas cattle drive is not exactly a place for softening up, and it seemed like I'd spent half my life getting along on less than nothing.

Hardship was a way of life to me, and there were few times when I wasn't hungry, cold, or fighting rough country for a living. Being snowed in up here in these mountains wasn't a pleasant thing, but some-how I'd survive. But those others now . . . ?

When I got back to camp the horses were close around the cave. I brought them inside and wiped them off. Mostly I fussed over them to keep their spir-its up. They were smart enough to know we were in trouble, but being cared for made them confident that all was well.

I wished I could be so sure myself.

When I had my fire going I took off my sheepskin coat and shed my vest before putting the coat back on. I always try to have a little something extra to put on when out in cold weather. Main thing a man has to avoid is sweating. When he stops moving that sweat can freeze into an icy sheet inside the clothes.

I fixed myself some grub, and sat by the fire with Blackstone open. Time to time, I'd squint in the fire-light to make something out.

These last few months, after I went to bed, some-times I'd lie awake into the night, a-contemplating things I'd read, or trying to say things, using the words taken from that book. By the time spring came I had hoped my talking would be better.

And, time to time, I had thought of Ange... About the time I was doing for her and she was half-dead from starvation and exhaustion, when I thought maybe this was my woman. I spent a sight of time daydreaming around, just contemplating her, and all about her.

But there wasn't much left to think about. She'd made that plain the other night in the store. Might have been better to let Kitch shoot me. Only I didn't believe that. I've heard of men killing themselves over a woman—most fool thing I ever heard tell of.

Women are practical. They get right down to bedrock about things, and no woman is going to waste much time remembering a man who was fool enough to kill himself. Thing to do is live for love, not die for it.

Though most womenfolks would a sight rather see a man dead than with another woman.

Only that evening alone, with the fire bright in the cave, I got something all bunched up in my throat, just a-wishing and a-dreaming over Ange and that red-gold hair.

After I'd eaten, I packed a bait of grub for morning, fixed over my snowshoes a mite, and settled down for the night, stowing the book away in my saddlebag.

A good hour before suntime I rolled out of my soogan and stowed it away. I fixed myself some breakfast and went down to the creek with the horses. Breaking a hole with my axe, I watered them there. I knocked some grass free of snow and ice, but it wasn't enough... the day wasn't long enough to get enough.

Strapping on the snowshoes and slinging a pack, I took a length of rope and my Winchester and started out. It was shy of daybreak when I reached the trail into the canyon.

The first thing I saw was a smear on the snow of the trail, almost halfway down. Something had fallen on the trail.

Carefully, using handholds on the rock wall where I could find them, I started down the trail, and when I got to the smear I could see a little snow had already blown over it. So it must have happened during the night. And whatever it was had fallen over the edge.

I edged close to the rim. Here and there the wind had piled the snow until it had built up a cornice. If a man should rest his weight on it, down he would go. Leaning over, I looked down.

It was Ange.

She was lying on a ledge maybe twenty feet down. Snow had blown over her. That red-gold hair lay like a flame on the snow, caught in the first light that filtered through the dawn clouds.

Putting my rifle down, I hunted around, till I found a mess of bristle-cone roots exposed by a slide. I knotted my rope to them and went over the side, landing beside her in a shower of snow. The ledge on which she lay was deep in snow and not over six or seven feet across, and maybe three times that long.

She was not dead.

I picked her up in my arms and held her close, trying to get her warm, and whispered all sorts of nonsense to her.

I tied a bowline around her body under her arms, snug enough so she couldn't slip through. Then, hand over hand, clambering for footholds in the rock, I pulled myself back up to the trail. When I had caught my breath, I hoisted her up.

By the time I had her on the trail it was day and there was plenty of light. Unknotting the bowline, I coiled my rope, strapped on my snowshoes, and picked her up. She had a bad knot on her head, but the thickness of her hair and the snow had probably cushioned the blow, so I doubted if she was hurt much.

I hadn't taken two steps before I heard a shout, far below, and a rifle shot that must have been very low, because it came nowhere near me. I turned, and saw several black figures against the snow of the canyon, far below.

Ange stirred, and opened her eyes. Quickly, pulling back as far as I could against the cliff wall, I put her down on her feet.

"Tell? Tell, is it really you? I thought—"

"You all right?"

"I fell . . . I thought I fell over the edge."

"You did." Rifle in one hand, and her hand in the other, I eased along the trail, hugging the rocks. Another shot put a bullet close to me, and I could see men running for the trail's end. One of them fell, but the others did not stop.

"Who is it down there?"

"It's Mr. Tuthill and those others. Ira Bigelow and Tom. That man named Boyd and two others I don't know. One of them they call Ben."

Ben Hobes?

"They made me bring them, Tell. They threatened

me. Besides . . . you hadn't come back and I was afraid."

It was growing colder. The clouds were breaking and the wind was mounting. It was slow going because of the ice beneath the snow. At the top of the trail, I got out of the snowshoes and tied them on Ange.

I thought back to the men who by now were making their way up the trail. There were six men down there, and they wanted the gold; but most of all, they wanted to kill me. Under the circumstances, they must kill Ange, too.

"Who knows you came with them?"

"Nobody does. Mr. Tuthill heard us talking, and he must have known about the gold already. But from what I said to you, he could tell that I knew about it too. He came to my cabin and offered to become my partner and get all the gold for us. I refused.

"He went away, and then when it was dark he came back with those other men. He told me to get dressed, and to dress warmly. He said he would kill me if I didn't . . . and he meant it.

"I had no idea what he intended to do until we were outside. And then I found out what had happened. They tried to follow you, and you got away from them, so they came back after me.

"The only way I knew was back the way we came out, and I was not very sure of that. When we got in the mountains it was turning colder and the rain was falling. We got to the cave, and by that time, they were half-frozen and arguing among themselves.

"Boyd stayed on watch, but he fell asleep and I slipped out. I knew you were up here somewhere."

We struggled through the snow, with her talking fast, nervous and scared. "Tell, they mean to kill you. I was wrong, Tell! I didn't understand what kind of men they were!"

The fire was down to the merest coals when we got to the cave. From my stacked fuel I built up the fire to warm the place, and put some snow on to melt for coffee water.

When I looked up from the fire, Ange was standing there looking at me. "Tell, I'm sorry. I didn't understand."

"What could you think? I just up and shot those men. Of course, they were hunting it. They figured to kill me. I'm sorry you had to see it."

I walked to the opening and looked out. The sky was bright, the air was sharp with cold, but there was no sign of Tuthill and the others.

"Back east," I said, "folks still have duels now and again, only they arrange them . . . everything all laid out pretty and conducted like a ceremony. Only difference is that out here we don't bother with fixing it up proper. Back where most every man is known, it's different. Out here most of us are strangers and nobody knows if the man he has a difficulty with is a gentleman, or not. So he just ups and shoots."

"That's what Joe told me. I . . . I wouldn't listen at first. It seemed so . . . so brutal."

"Yes, ma'am. It is brutal. Only I never could see the sense in having folks look at your tombstone and say, 'He was a man who didn't believe in violence. He's a good man . . . and dead.' "

I paused, peering at the trees opposite. "No, Ange, if the folks who believe in law, justice, and a decent life for folks are to be shot down by those who believe in violence, nothing makes much sense. I believe in justice, I believe in being tolerating of other folks, but I pack a big pistol, ma'am, and will use it when needed."

There was no sign of those men yet. Either they were having trouble on the trail, or they were Injuning up on me and would settle down to shooting most any time. The snow and ice had covered the piles of waste rock thrown out of the tunnel so it wasn't likely they would guess first off that this was where the mine was.

Ange saw my Blackstone and picked it up. "Are you studying this?" She looked up at me curiously.

"Yes, ma'am. It's books like that which make a man proud of being a man."

"Are you going to be a lawyer?"

"No . . . my brother Orrin made himself into one, but Orrin always was a talker. He had the gift, the Welsh tongue. I don't have any gift, ma'am, I'm just a man tries to do the right thing as well as he knows. Only, the way I figure, no man has the right to be ignorant. In a country like this, ignorance is a crime. If a man is going to vote, if he's going to take part in his country and its government, then it's up to him to understand.

"I had no schooling, ma'am, so I'm making out with this book and a few others. Some day"—I felt myself getting red around the gills—"I hope to have children and they'll have schooling, and I don't aim they should be ashamed of their Pa."

"How could they be?" Ange demanded. "You're good, you're brave, and—"

"Here they come," I said, and settled down behind the woodpile.

We could hear their boots crunching through the snow. There were five of them. Tuthill I recognized at once, and the two men beside him were probably the Bigelows. Will Boyd looked done up from the climbing and the cold. Behind him was Ben Hobes. The only one missing was that white-haired youngster with the guns.

I watched them come, chewing on a bit of stick, my Winchester in my hands. They were playing the fool, for at that distance . . .

"Come on out, Sackett! We want to talk."

"I can hear you."

"Come on out here."

"And leave this warm fire? I'm comfortable."

They started arguing among themselves. Then Tuthill started toward the cave, so I put a bullet into the snow at his feet and he stopped so quick he almost fell.

"You boys have got bigger problems than me," I commented, conversationally. "A sight of snow fell since you came into the mountains. How do you plan to get out?"

"Look here, Sackett," Tuthill said, "we know you're sitting on a rich claim. Well, all we want is a piece of it. Why be foolish? There's enough for us all."

"Why share it? I've got it, and all you boys have got is a chance to die in the snow."

I eased my position a little. "Tuthill, you don't seem to understand. When you came in here you came into a trap. The passes are closed, and we're all going to spend the winter. I hope you brought grub for five or six months."

"If you don't come out, Sackett," Tuthill threatened, "we're coming in."

"If I shoot again, Tuthill, I'll shoot to kill."

It was cold. Knowing this kind of country as I did, I knew what we could expect. It had cleared off. It was cold now—at least ten below. In a few hours it might drop to fifty below.

"Ben," I called, "you're no pilgrim. Tell them how cold it can get at ten or eleven thousand feet on a still night. We are all stuck for the winter, and you might as well get used to the idea.

"You're going to need shelter, fuel, and food. The game won't stay this high, it will all head for lower ground. If you make a run for it, you might still get out."

The pile of firewood covered half the tunnel mouth to a height of more than four feet, and made a crude windbreak and shelter from gunfire. The tunnel, in following the vein, had taken a slight bend—enough to shelter one person—and I whispered to Ange to get back behind it.

While partly open, the walls of rock acted as reflectors and threw heat back upon us. Moreover, in our struggle to live, I would have three priceless assets not available to them—the pick, shovel, and axe.

They had come to take a mine away from me. I had come to work the mine.

I knew there were at least two things they could do that would be terribly dangerous to us. They could direct a heavy fire at the walls and roof of the tunnel, causing the bullets to ricochet within the small space.

Such bullets tear like the jagged pieces of hot metal they are.

And they could kill the horses.

Killing them in the tunnel mouth could obscure our vision, and might even block escape. It might be they were doomed to die anyway, but I was going to get them out if I could.

Somewhere up on the slope a tree branch cracked in the cold. It was very still . . . an icy stillness.

Boyd stamped his feet and complained. Boyd would be the first to go. He simply hadn't the guts for the long pull. Of them all, Ben Hobes was the one to last.

Suddenly, they turned around and started for the trees. *I should nail one of them,* I thought. Then it was too late, and they were under three large trees and behind some brush where I could hear branches breaking as they built a fire. They would need more than a fire.

Where was the kid?

There had been six . . . one had tripped and fallen down below. That whole lower canyon was a vast snare of boulders and logs, covered now with snow.

The bullet hit the butt end of a cut log just an instant before the report racketed against the hills. I reached over for the coffeepot and filled my cup. Nursing it in my hands to keep my fingers warm, I sat tight. A volley of shots came next, and one of them struck above the entrance, showering the woodpile with chipped rock.

"Stay back there, Ange. Don't move unless you have to."

"Tell? Are we going to get out of this?"

"Ange, I could lie to you, but I don't know. If any of us get out, we'll be lucky."

For several minutes they kept up a hammering fire and I let them shoot, holding my cup in my hands and waiting. Finally, they stopped, and we could hear them arguing.

Would they believe us dead? That was what I hoped.

Tuthill called out, but I made no sound. A couple of searching shots came then, one striking the rock above the opening again, the other hitting just inside.

Again Tuthill yelled, and I finished my coffee, peering through openings in the woodpile.

Another shot. This one struck deep into the cave with an angry smack.

There was more arguing. The voices could be heard, but not the words. Then the bushes parted and Tom Bigelow was coming toward the cave, a pistol in his hand.

He slowed as he came nearer, worried by what he was doing. He paused, threw up his pistol, and fired. It was a quick, testing shot, and it struck the rock at the side of the opening.

Bigelow hesitated, then came on, walking fast. He was within a dozen steps when I spoke out. "All right, Bigelow. Drop that gun!"

He pulled up sharp, starting to tilt the gun.

"Drop it!"

He could see the rifle muzzle now. At that distance even a child couldn't miss with a Winchester. He dropped the gun.

"Your brother was killed because he tried to bottom deal on me, and I told him he'd better not grab iron. He tried it. I didn't want to kill him."

Tom Bigelow said nothing.

"Unloose your gun belt," I said.

He unfastened the belt and let it fall.

"All right, I'm letting you go back. But before you go, you might tell me what you boys are going to do for something to eat. Your passes are closed. You can't take our grub, and if you could, there isn't enough to last out a week."

"We can get back."

"Ask Ben Hobes. Ask him about Al Packer."

"Who's he?"

"He started across the mountains in the winter with a party. They ran out of grub. He ate all five of the others. These same mountains. Are you ready for that, Bigelow?"

"You're lyin'!"

"All right, go on back."

One less gun they had, and maybe eighteen to twenty less ca'tridges. Come nighttime they would try and close in on me. Of course, on the white snow . . .

"Did they bring any packhorses?" I asked Ange.

"No," she said, "they planned to go right back."

They would be short of grub then. Whatever they did, they must do at once.

Suddenly, as Bigelow disappeared into the trees, I levered three fast, searching shots over there, waited an instant, then fired again, holding the rifle a little lower.

Shivering, I added fuel to the fire. The hungry flames crept slowly along the branches, then finding a piece of pitch pine, blazed up. A shot struck the roof, richocheted down, and scattered fire. I brushed the sparks from my clothing and the bed, and felt a sharp tug at my sleeve as a second bullet came, striking just beyond the fire.

Through the trees I could see their fire. Lying prone on the cold floor, and taking my time, I drew a careful bead on a dark spot at the edge. It might be a log or a stump. It might also be a man.

For a moment I relaxed. Then, taking a long breath, I gathered trigger-slack, let the breath out slowly, and squeezed off the shot.

The cry was hoarse, choking . . . followed by a horrible retching sound such as I had never heard from anything, animal or human.

There was a volley in reply. I fired four more shots that covered an area about four feet back from the fire, and then a final shot across the fire itself.

"Ange," I said, "you'll find some cold flour in my pack. Take it and some of that meat and cook them up together. When it gets dark, we're going to get out."

"Can we?"

"We can try."

Worried as I was about what Tuthill and the rest of them might do, I was more worried about the cold.

Somehow we had to escape. We had to try. We had to try while we had our strength.

Ange was in no condition to attempt a winter in the mountains. We lacked the food for it, lacked the proper clothing and equipment. Yet bad off as we were, those others must be suffering more by now. For his own sake, I hoped the man I shot was dead.

Frightened by the firing, the horses had drawn away from the cave mouth. Now they started back, but before they could reach us, two quick shots put them down. The packhorse first, then the appaloosa.

For the first time in months I swore. Pa was never strong on cussing, and Ma was dead set against it, so we boys kind of grew up without doing much of that, but I said some words this time. They were good horses, and they had done no harm to anyone. But I knew why they were killed. Those men over there, they were realizing how much they needed grub . . . and horse meat was still meat, and not bad eating at that.

Night came. Stars appeared, wind came flowing like icy water over the rim of the mountain. The moon was not visible to us yet, but shone white upon the mountain tops. Twice I dusted the woods with gunfire; and then Ange and me, we ate what we could. What was left of the jerked meat I stowed away in a pack, and made another pack of our blankets and the ammunition.

With a long pole I'd used a couple of times for fishing, I reached out and snagged Tom Bigelow's gun belt, then the pistol. I shucked the shells from the gun belt, and used them to fill empty loops in my own belt. Emptying the shells into my hand from the cylinder, I took my axe and smashed the firing pin.

Then I made a loop on my pack from which to hang the axe, and covered over the shovel and pick with rock waste from the floor of the tunnel. They would probably find them, but I had no intention of making anything easy.

Occasionally a shot hit the back wall or struck into the woodpile. Only at long intervals I returned their fire . . . I wanted them to become accustomed to long waiting.

There was every chance they would try an attack under cover of darkness, although their dark figures would be visible on the snow for a time. However if they managed to cross far down the valley and worked toward us along the wall . . .

"Be ready to move," I whispered to Ange. "I think they will try something now, and after that we're pulling out."

Getting up from behind the stacked wood, I moved outside and eased along the rock wall until I could look both ways. Nothing at first . . . then a faint whisper of coarse cloth brushing on branches. Waiting until I detected a movement, I lifted the rifle, located the movement again, and fired.

There was a grunt, a heavy fall, and a bullet struck rock near my face. I ducked and half fell back into the tunnel. Outside there was cursing, and several shots. Catching up the packs, I slung one on my back. Ange already had the small one. An instant we paused. I levered a shot at a stab of flame from the trees, and then we slipped out.

The area around the tunnel lay in heavy darkness. We went swiftly along the wall and, when well away from the tunnel, turned up through the trees.

We had to go down the trail up which they had come, and go down it in darkness. Then we had to go up the opposite side, climb that steep talus slope to the bare, icy ridge that overlooked the Vallecitos. Whether Ange could make this, I did not know.

Once into the trees and moving, working away from the valley of the mine, we slowed down, holding to a steady pace. The snow had frozen, and we moved now across a good surface where there was no need for snowshoes.

The crude pair had been abandoned, as they were in bad shape anyway after the rough usage they had. As long as the cold held the snow would remain solid, but when it began to get warmer the ice beneath the snow, left from the sleet storm, would melt. Once that happened, travel would become impossible. At the lightest step, snow might slide, bringing down all the snow upon an entire mountainside in one gigantic avalanche. The cold was a blessing, severe as it was.

We traveled steadily. Nobody would be too anxious to investigate the mine, even when they began to believe we had escaped. And when they did investigate, they would start at once to seek for gold. Most of that in sight had been taken by me, and they were going to have to do some digging to get at the rest.

And before long they would have other things on their minds.

Time to time I stopped to give Ange a chance to catch her breath and ease her muscles. She didn't complain, and seemed to be holding up.

The moon was bright on the canyon wall when we came to the path down. Ange caught my sleeve. "Tell? Do we have to?"

"We have to."

I tried a foot on the trail. The frozen snow might make it a lot easier going down than loose snow over that sleet. Moving carefully, like a man walking on eggs, I started down.

Wind bit at exposed flesh, stiffening our muscles. The canyon below was a great open mouth of darkness. Above us the ridges and peaks towered pure, white, and glittering with wild beauty in the moonlight. It's rare in a man's life to see such a sight, and I stopped for a minute, just taking it in. Ange was standing close behind, her hands on my back.

"I wish Ma could see that," I said. "She favors lovely things."

The wind gnawed at our faces with icy teeth, as we moved along. Snow crunched as we put our feet down, each step a lifetime of risk and doubt.

The path was scarce three feet wide, widening to four at the most but looking broader in spots because of the cornices of snow that hung over the lip. It was a steep path where every step had to be separate, the foot put carefully down, the weight rested gradually, and then the other foot lifted.

The sky above was amazingly bright; the moon made the hills and peaks like day. High above, on a frosty ridge where I hoped to be by daylight, the snow blew, throwing a brief veil across the sky. The snow hanging on the slopes above the trail made me mighty uneasy. Snow like that can start to slide on the slightest provocation, and with daylight it would become worse.

When we were halfway down, we stopped again, and Ange came up beside me. "You ready for it?" I asked her. "They'll be coming soon, Ange."

"How long has it been?"

"Couple of hours . . ."

We hit bottom with our knees shaking, and headed for the cave. By daylight they would realize we were gone. With the fire out, they would soon guess that we'd lit a shuck, and they would come a-helling after us.

We were almost to the cave before we smelled smoke. Catching a whiff of it, I pulled up short. Somebody was in the cave.

Stepping into the opening, gun up and ready, I found myself looking into the muzzle of a .44 gun. That gun muzzle looked as great as the cave mouth, as black as death itself.

"Mister," I said, "you put down that .44 gun. If you don't, I'm sure going to kill you."

And all the while he had the drop on me.

CHAPTER 14

KID NEWTON WAS holding that pistol—that white headed kid I'd talked out of trouble back down the line.

He was lying on his back, looking sick, and the gun in his hand was shaky. A blanket was pulled over him, and I could see from the fire that he had been feeding sticks into it without getting up.

"What's the matter, Kid? You in trouble?"

He kept the gun on me. Could I swing that Winchester up in time to nail him? I was hoping I wouldn't have to try.

"Busted my leg."

"And they left you? That ain't hardly decent, Kid." Using up all the nerve I had in store, I put my rifle down. "Kid, put that gun away and let me look at your leg."

"You got no cause to help me," he said, but I could see he wanted help more than anybody I'd ever seen.

"You're hurt, that's cause enough. Maybe when you get well I'll have cause to shoot you, but right now I wouldn't leave no man in your kind of trouble."

I said to Ange, "You stay in the opening and keep a lookout. We may have to shoot our way out of here yet."

Taking the pistol from his hand, I pulled back the

blanket. He had made a try at splinting his leg, but the splints had come loose. The leg was swollen and looked a fright.

I cut a split in his pants leg, and cut his boot to get it off. No cowhand likes to have a good pair of boots ruined, but there was no other way about it. Looked like a clean break a few inches below the knee, but those splints had been a lousy job. I cut some fresh ones, then I made a try at doing something to ease him.

I heated some water, and put hot cloths on that leg. To tell the truth, I wasn't sure how much good they'd do, but they would make him think he was being helped, a comfort to a man that's been lying alone, half-froze to death in a lonely cave.

"You drag yourself here?"

"They left me."

"That's a rawhide outfit, Kid. They aren't worth shootin'. You ought to cut loose from them and line up with a real bunch."

Breaking some sticks, I built up the fire, and all the time I was thinking what a pickle we were in. We had it bad enough, Ange and me, trying to take out over that ridge. And as if we weren't in trouble enough, we were now saddled with a man with a broke . . . broken leg.

Folks might say it was none of my business, that my first duty was to get Ange out of here, and myself. It was nip and tuck whether we would make it or not—I'd say we were on the short end of the odds. The Kid had come with men who intended to rob me, probably murder me. And before that he had tried to pick a fight with me. Someday, somebody was going to have to shoot him, more than likely.

But left here, he would freeze to death before he could starve. There was no two ways about that. And none of that gold-hungry crowd would lift a hand to help.

Taking the axe, I walked down to the trees. The moon was gone now, but day was not too far off. Searching through a bunch of second-growth timber, stuff that had grown up after a slide had ripped it down, I found in a thick cluster of aspen just what I wanted, and cut two slim poles about eight feet long.

I carried them back to the cave, after trimming the branches off, and then took the axe and smoothed off one side. My axe was sharp and I'd split enough rails for fences back in Tennessee to know how to trim up a young tree. On the bottom end I made a bevel, curving the end upward a mite.

Going to the woodpile, I cut some crosspieces, notched the poles to take four of them, and then fitted them into the notches.

"What you fixin'?"

"You set quiet. Can't pack you out of here on my back, so I'm fixing a toboggan . . . such as it is."

"You'd take me out of here?" The Kid was not expecting any favors, seemed like.

"Can't let you lie here and freeze," I told him irritably. "Best thing you can do is stay quiet. If we get out at all, you'll be with us, but don't get your hopes up. Our chances are mighty poor."

For several minutes, while I wove some rawhide around the crosspieces, Kid Newton had nothing to say. Finally, he eased his leg a mite. "Sackett, you and that girl better take out. I mean, I'm no account. Why, I was fixin' to kill you back along the trail."

"Kid, you'd never have cleared leather. I wasn't hunting trouble, but I cut my teeth on a six-shooter."

"You can make it, you two. You're never going to get me over any trail on that sled."

"We aren't going by trail." I sat back on my heels. "Kid, if you get out of this alive you can sure tell folks you've been up the creek and over the mountain, because that's where we're going."

He didn't get it. And reason enough he couldn't. No man in his right mind would try what I figured to do.

Some of the trails by which we had come into the mountains would by now be a dozen feet under the snow. What I figured to do was go over the ridge . . . to go right down the steep side of the mountain into camp.

Crazy? Sure . . . but the chute was choked with snow and ice, the upper valley was full by now, and the other trails, the one by which Ange came in . . . the passes would be choked with snow there.

We had all come in on horseback, but no horse could get out. In places the snow might carry the weight of a man alone, but never the weight of men and horses. We might make it out, but it was a risk scarcely worth thinking about.

It is one thing to ride a horse through unknown country; it is another to go back afoot. It would take twice, maybe three times as long. The gang up there had figured to come in and go right out. . . .

"What do you mean?" The Kid was looking at me now like he was afraid he did know.

Pausing in my work, I gestured at the mountain opposite. "The one above us is higher, and we're going over it."

He knew I was crazy now. One lone man taking a girl and a wounded man over that mountain!

The sky was gray overhead when we started out of there, me towing that crude toboggan behind me. The slope of talus was steep, but easier going with the snow on it, for the rock did not slide under me. Still, it was a struggle to get up to the foot of that chimney.

Ange looked up at it, and her eyes were mighty big when she turned back to me. "Tell," she whispered, "you can't do it. It's impossible."

To tell the truth, I didn't feel very good about it myself. That was a high mountain, and that climb was going to be something. Slinging my rifle around my shoulders and hanging a coil of rope to my belt, I told Ange to come on.

The Kid, he was tied onto that sled, and he laid there looking at me. "You going to leave me, Sackett? I don't blame you. Unless you can fly, you ain't going up there."

I made one end of the rope fast to the head of the toboggan, and got ready to climb. The rope was made fast by taking a round turn on each runner, then tying the end of the rope to the standing part, so the sled would hang straight when I started to pull it.

Going up ahead, I cut a few toeholds in the ice, and found a couple I'd used before where no ice had collected. When at last I climbed the chimney, I guided Ange.

She was little, but mighty lithe and strong when it

came right down to it, and she made easier work of that climb up the chimney than I had.

The old, gnarled bristle-cone was standing there where I'd remembered it, atop that chimney and rooted deep in the rock. Taking a turn around that old tree, I dug my heels in and started to hand over hand that rope. Like I said, I'm a big man with a lot of beef in my shoulders and arms, but when I took the strain of that full weight, I surely knew I was in trouble.

Getting him clear of the ground was only part of it. He had to fend himself off the rocky face with his hands. A time or two, I could feel him helping me where he could get a handhold.

Ange stood behind me and cleared the rope around the trunk of the pine so we could hold what we had got. My hands were stiff, and I didn't think I'd ever get my fingers unwound from about that rope. But I hauled away.

Stopping to rest myself, with the Kid hanging there like a papoose slung on a packboard, I looked off across the valley.

Somebody was coming down the trail. How far? Maybe a quarter of a mile, a bit more or less. There were only four of them, the man behind was making a slow thing of it.

One of them jerked up his rifle and we heard the sound of a shot. What happened to that bullet I never could say, but it came nowhere near us. Judging distance across a canyon like that, when the target is higher than you—that's quite a stunt. Why, I've missed a few shots like that my own self.

Digging in my heels, I took hold of that rope. My

arms ached and I was fighting for breath. Those high-up ridges surely took a man's wind. But I got him up a couple of feet farther, beat my hands to warm them, and started at it again.

There was no time to look across the canyon. There was only time to haul away. Heave, and heave again . . . catch a breath, and heave again.

Then the toboggan brought up against something and stuck.

"Ange," I said, straightening up, "I'm going down. When I clear the sled, you get as much rope around that pine as can be."

"Tell?"

Turning around, I looked at her. She was looking right at me. "Why are you doing this? Is it because of the way I acted?"

Well, I declare! I hadn't thought of that. "No, Ange, I never gave thought to that. No man can abide much by what a woman thinks, at times like this. He does what it's his nature to do. That man down there . . . we had words one time. He was figuring to shoot me, and I was planning to beat him to it.

"That there's one thing, this here's another. That's a helpless man, and when I get him up here and get him safe, then maybe he'll come a-gunning for me. So I'll have to shoot him."

I started down the slope, then stopped and looked back. "Seems a lot of trouble to go to, doesn't it?"

Well, I cleared him, and we hoisted him out on top of the ridge, using the same route I'd found on that day when I left Ange in the cave.

Down below was Cap, our log house, and our claim—down there in those trees. And up here the wind was blowing a gale, and a man could scarcely stand erect. One thing I knew: we had to get off that mountain, and fast.

It was clouding up again—great banks of gray, solid cloud. That could mean more snow. That canyon could be twenty feet deep in snow before the week was out.

Camp was a half-mile as the crow flies, but a good five thousand feet down. Looking north to where I'd spotted what looked like a way down, I could still see it, despite the snow. Once into the trees, we could make it all right, although it would be work.

This ridge was about thirteen thousand feet up, and the wind was roaring along it. All the gray granite was swept clean, although there were flurries of snow in the air from time to time. Leaning into the wind, we started on, towing the sled. Finally we got down over the edge of the ridge. Right away, the wind seemed to let up.

My face was raw from the wind, my hands were numb. My fingers in their gloves felt stiff, and I was afraid that the Kid, held immovable the way he was, would freeze to death.

Lowering the sled away ahead of us, we made it down. One time the wind came around a shoulder of the mountain and lifted the sled, man and all, like it was a leaf, but set it down again before the rope tore from my hands. We both heard the Kid scream when the drop jolted his broken leg.

Bracing myself on great shattered rocks, I lowered him. Climbing after, lowering Ange, I lost all sense of time, and could not remember when it ever had been warm.

Below us was a huge old tree, ripped from the rock by its roots. It sprawled like a great spider, petrified in the moment of death, legs writhing. A little below it were some wind-tortured trees, and then the forest. We could see the tops of the trees and, far off below, a white, white world of snow, with here and there a faint feather of smoke rising from some house.

Hugging that wind-torn mountainside, and looking down into those treetops, I could hardly believe there was a house with a fire burning in it, or Ma a-rocking in her old rocker, or Orrin a-singing. It was a world far away from the wind, the cold, and snow that drove at your face like sand.

But, easing the sled down a little farther, we got into the trees. From there to the bottom it was mostly a matter of guiding the sled, belaying the rope around a tree here and there to ease it, and working our way through. One time Ange almost dropped, and my own knees were buckling most of the way.

By the time we reached the path I'd cut to build a little fort above the camp, I had fallen down a couple of times, and I was so numb with cold and so exhausted I could scarce think. The draw rope over my shoulder, and one arm around Ange, I started through the tall pines toward the house.

The snow was deep under the trees, but there was a slow lift of smoke from the chimney, and a light in the window. Seemed like only a short time ago it was coming daylight, and now it was nighttime again.

Then I fell, face down in the snow. Seemed to me I tried to get up . . . seemed to get my hands under me and push. I could see that light in the window and I could hear myself talking. I hauled away and got to the door, where I couldn't make my fingers work the latch.

The door opened of a sudden and Cap was standing there with a six-gun in his hand, looking like he was the old Cap and ready to start shooting.

"It ain't worth the trouble, Cap. I think I'm dead already."

Joe Rugger was there, and between them they got Kid Newton off the sled and into the house. Ange, she just sat down and started to cry, and I knelt on the floor and put my arm around her and kept telling her everything was all right.

Kid Newton caught my sleeve. "By God," he said, "today I seen a man! I thought—"

"Get some sleep," I said. "Joe's going for the doctor."

"I seen a man," the Kid repeated. "Why, when I hung those guns on me I thought I was something, I thought—"

"Shut up," I said. And I reached my hands toward the fire a distance off. I could feel the million tiny needles starting to dance in my fingers as the cold began to leave them.

"Speaking of men"—I looked over at Newton—"if you ever get down to Mora, I've got two brothers down there, Tyrel and Orrin. Now there's a couple of men!

"Always figured to make something of myself," I said, "but I guess I just ain't got in me."

Sitting on the edge of the bed, I just let the heat soak into me, every muscle feeling stretched out and useless. Ange had quit her crying and dropped off to sleep there beside me, her face drawn, dark hollows under her eyes.

"You been through it," Cap said. He looked at Newton. "What did you bring him back for?"

"I got no better sense, Cap. I brought him down off that mountain because there was nobody else to do it."

"But he wanted to kill you!"

"Sure . . . he had him a notion, that was all. I reckon since then he's had time to contemplate."

Cap Rountree took his pipe out of his teeth and dumped coffee in the pot.

"Then you take time to contemplate about this," he said. "There's another Bigelow down in town. He's asking for you."

CHAPTER 15

IT WASN'T IN me to lie abed. Come daylight, I was on my feet, but I wasn't up to much. What I really got up for was vittles. Seemed like I hadn't been so hungry in years.

Ange was still sleeping in the other room, and Joe Rugger and his wife, just out from Ohio, had come out to the place.

"That Bigelow worries me," Rugger said. "He's a man hunting trouble like you never saw."

"Those Bigelows," I said, "they remind me of those little animals a Swede told me about one time. Called them lemmings or something like that. Seems as if all of a sudden they take out for the ocean . . . millions of them, and they run right into the ocean and drown. Those Bigelows seem bound and determined to get themselves killed just as fast as they can manage."

"Don't take him lightly, Tell," Rugger warned me. "He killed a man in Denver City, and another in Tascosa. Benson Bigelow, he's the oldest, biggest, and toughest of all of them."

"Heard of him," Cap said. "I didn't know he was kin."

"He's been asking questions about his brothers. They haven't come back out of the mountains, and he says you murdered them."

"Them and three more? That's quite a lot to take on. Believe me, they haven't come out of the mountains, and it will surprise me if they ever do."

The warmth of the room felt good and after a while I stretched out and slept some more.

When I opened my eyes Ange was fixing something at the stove. I got up and pulled on my boots. I spilled some water in the basin and washed my face and hands. The water felt good on my face, and I decided I needed a shave.

Cap was off somewhere, and just the two of us were there. The doctor had taken the Kid away. It was nice, shaving, with Ange fussing over something at the fire. Finally she called me to dinner and I was ready. Cap came in, stomping the snow from his boots on the stoop.

"Snowing," he said. "You were lucky. A few hours more, and you might never have made it."

Ange brought me a cup of coffee and I held it in my hands, thinking about those men up there. They brought it on themselves, and despite their ill feeling for me, I was wishing they would make it.

They never did.

Cap accepted coffee too, and he looked over at me. "That Benson Bigelow is telling it around that you're yellow, afraid to meet him."

Some folks are bound and determined to make fools of themselves.

All I wanted was a ranch of my own, some cattle, and a little land I could crop. Only when I looked up there at Ange I knew that wasn't all I wanted.

I had no idea how to put it, and hated to risk it, knowing how little I had to offer. Here I was a grown man, just learning to read proper, and although I'd found some gold there was no telling how deep that vein would run. In fact, it acted to me like a pocket. That was why as soon as spring came I was going to light out for Mora to see the boys.

I said as much to Cap.

"You needn't worry," he said. "Tyrel and Orrin, they're riding up here. Them and Ollie Shaddock."

Ollie was from the Cumberland too. Sheriff back there one time, and some kin of ours. He was the one who got Orrin into politics, although Tennessee boys take to politics like they do to coon hunting.

"When do you expect them?"

"Tonight or tomorrow, if all goes well. They heard you were fetching trouble and they sent word they were coming up."

They would ride into town and, unknown to them, that Bigelow would be there, and he might hear one of them called Sackett and just open up and start shooting.

If he faced them, I wasn't worried. Tyrel now, Tyrel was hell on wheels with a pistol.

I finished my coffee and got up. Then I took down my gun belt and slung it around my hips and took down my coat and hat. "Riding up to town," I said. "A little fresh air."

"Kind of stuffy in here," Cap Rountree said. "Mind if I ride along?"

Ange had turned from the fire with a big spoon in her hand.

"What about supper? After I've gone to all this trouble?"

"We'll be back," I said. "You keep it warm, Ange."

I shrugged into my coat and put on my hat. I was going to have to get me a coonskin for this weather. "Anyway," I said, "the way I figure, I shouldn't get used to your cooking, nohow. A man can form a habit."

She was looking me right in the eye, her face flushed a mite from the fire, looking pretty as all get-out.

"Trouble is, no woman in her right mind would marry a fool, and I'm certainly one."

"A lot you know about women!" she scoffed. "Did you ever see a fool who didn't have a wife?"

Come to that, I hadn't.

"Keep it warm," I said.

She didn't say a word about shooting or Benson Bigelow. She just said, "You come back, Tell Sackett, I won't have my supper wasted. Not after all this trouble."

It was cool in the outside air, and Cap led the horses out. He had them saddled. "Figured you wouldn't want the boys to come up against it, unexpected," he said.

The saloon was hot and crowded, and up at the bar a big man was standing. He had a broad, hard-boned face and it took only one look to see this was no ordinary Bigelow, this was the Old Man of the Woods, right from Bitter Creek, tough and mean and not all talk.

He turned around and looked at me and I walked over and leaned on the bar alongside him.

You never saw a saloon lose customers so fast. Must have been fifty, sixty men in there when I leaned on that bar, and a half minute later there weren't but five or six, the kind who just have to stay and see what happens, men determined to be innocent bystanders.

This Bigelow sized me up and I looked back at him kind of mild and round-eyed, and I said, "Nice mustache you have there, Mr. Bigelow."

"What's wrong with my mustache?"

"Why, nothing . . . exactly."

"What's that mean?"

"Buy you a drink?"

"What's wrong with my mustache? No, I'll buy my own drinks!"

For the first time he realized the crowd was gone. The skin under his eyes seemed to tighten.

Outside I thought I could hear horses coming. It was late for travel in this weather, which made me wonder if it wasn't Tyrel and Orrin.

Those brothers of mine . . . ride hundreds of miles—well, maybe a couple hundred—through rough country because they figured I was standing alone against trouble.

"Are you Tell Sackett?"

"That brother of yours, Wes, he never was no hand with cards. Nor a pistol, either."

"What happened to Tom and Ira?"

"You look long enough, you'll find them in the spring," I told him. "They had no more sense than to come chasing me back into the hills, with winter coming on and snow in the air."

"Did you see them?"

"They tried to kill me a couple of times. They weren't any better shots than Wes. Tom, he lost his gun up there."

Bigelow was quiet, and I could see him studying things out in his mind.

"Hear you came up here hunting me," I said mildly. "It's a long ride for the trouble."

He couldn't quite make me out. Nothing I had said showed I was troubled about anything, just talking like to any passerby.

"You know something, Bigelow? You better just straddle your horse and ride out of here. What happened to your brothers was brought on them by their own actions."

"Maybe you're right," he said. "I'll buy the drink."

So we had a drink together, and then I ordered one. When I got rid of that I drew back. "Well, I've got a good supper waiting for me. See you around, Bigelow."

Turning, I started for the door and then he said, "Sackett?"

His gun cocked when it cleared leather and a sound like that is plain to hear in an empty room. I drew as I turned and his first bullet whiffed by my ear. Steadying down, I shot him through the belly, and it slammed him against the bar. But he caught the edge with his left hand and pulled himself around. I did not hear the report, but I felt the slug take me low and hard. I braced myself and shot him again.

He did not go down . . . . .44 or not, you have to hit a man right through the heart, through the head, or on a big bone to stop him if he's mad, and Bigelow was killing mad. He was a big bear of a man and he looked tough as a winter on the caprock of west Texas.

For what seemed like minutes he stood there, and I could see the blood soaking his shirt front and pants, and then great red drops of it began to hit the floor between his feet.

He lifted his gun, taking his time, his left hand still clinging to the bar, and he took dead aim at me. He started to cock the gun, and I shot him again. He jolted the bar when he slammed against it. A bottle tipped over and rolled down the bar, spilling whiskey. He reached over and took up the bottle and drank out of it, holding it in his left hand, never taking his eyes off me.

He put the bottle down, and I said, "That drink was on me."

"I made a mistake," he said. "I guess you shot them honest."

"Only Wes . . . the cold got the others."

"All right," he said, and turned his back on me. I could hear running outside.

For a long minute I stood there with my gun in my hand looking at his back, and then his knees began to sag and he fell slowly, his fingers clinging as long as they could to the bar. Then he let go and rolled over on the floor and he was dead.

He lay there face up in the sawdust, his eyes open to the lights, and there was sawdust in his beard.

There was a wet feeling inside my pants where the blood was running down. I thumbed shells into my gun, holstered it, and Cap came up to me.

"You're hit," he said.

"Seems like," I said, and caught hold of the wall.

The door opened and Tyrel came in, with Orrin right behind him, both of them ready for trouble.

"We'd better get back to the place," I said. "Supper will get cold."

They looked past me at Bigelow.

"Any more of them?" Tyrel asked.

"If there are, they won't have to shoot me. I'll shoot myself."

Cap pulled my shirt open and they could see the blood oozing from a hole in the flesh over my hip. The bullet had cut itself a place without hitting a bone or doing much harm. Tyrel took out a silk handkerchief and plugged it up, and we went outside.

"The doctor's here," Cap protested. "You'd better see him."

"Bring him along. There's a lady waiting dinner."

When I came in the door of the cabin, Ange stood with her back to it. I could see her shoulders hunch a mite as if she expected to be hit, and I said, "This fool ain't married."

She turned around and looked at me. "He will be," she said, and dropped her spoon on the floor and came across the room and right into my arms.

So I taken her in my arms and for the first time in my life I had something that was really mine.

Seems like even a long, tall man who ain't much for looks can find him a woman, too.

About Louis L'Amour

*"I think of myself in the oral tradition—
as a troubadour, a village tale-teller, the man
in the shadows of the campfire. That's the way
I'd like to be remembered—as a storyteller.
A good storyteller."*

IT IS DOUBTFUL that any author could be as at
home in the world re-created in his novels as
Louis Dearborn L'Amour. Not only could he physically fill the boots of the rugged characters he wrote
about, but he literally "walked the land my characters walk." His personal experiences as well as his
lifelong devotion to historical research combined to
give Mr. L'Amour the unique knowledge and understanding of people, events, and the challenge of the
American frontier that became the hallmarks of his
popularity.

Of French-Irish descent, Mr. L'Amour could trace
his own family in North America back to the early
1600s and follow their steady progression westward,
"always on the frontier." As a boy growing up in
Jamestown, North Dakota, he absorbed all he could
about his family's frontier heritage, including the
story of his great-grandfather who was scalped by
Sioux warriors.

Spurred by an eager curiosity and a desire to

broaden his horizons, Mr. L'Amour left home at the age of fifteen and enjoyed a wide variety of jobs, including seaman, lumberjack, elephant handler, skinner of dead cattle, miner, and officer in the transportation corps during World War II. During his "yondering" days he also circled the world on a freighter, sailed a dhow on the Red Sea, was shipwrecked in the West Indies and stranded in the Mojave Desert. He won fifty-one of fifty-nine fights as a professional boxer and worked as a journalist and lecturer. He was a voracious reader and collector of rare books. His personal library contained 17,000 volumes.

Mr. L'Amour "wanted to write almost from the time I could talk." After developing a widespread following for his many frontier and adventure stories written for fiction magazines, Mr. L'Amour published his first full-length novel, *Hondo,* in the United States in 1953. Every one of his more than 120 books is in print; there are more than 300 million copies of his books in print worldwide, making him one of the bestselling authors in modern literary history. His books have been translated into twenty languages, and more than forty-five of his novels and stories have been made into feature films and television movies.

His hardcover bestsellers include *The Lonesome Gods, The Walking Drum* (his twelfth-century historical novel), *Jubal Sackett, Last of the Breed,* and *The Haunted Mesa.* His memoir, *Education of a Wandering Man,* was a leading bestseller in 1989. Audio dramatizations and adaptations of many L'Amour stories are available from Random House Audio publishing.

The recipient of many great honors and awards, in 1983 Mr. L'Amour became the first novelist ever to be awarded the Congressional Gold Medal by the United States Congress in honor of his life's work. In 1984 he was also awarded the Medal of Freedom by President Reagan.

Louis L'Amour died on June 10, 1988. His wife, Kathy, and their two children, Beau and Angelique, carry the L'Amour publishing tradition forward with new books written by the author during his lifetime to be published by Bantam.

FORGET THE LAW OF THE JUNGLE...

The Worst
Drought In
Memory . . .

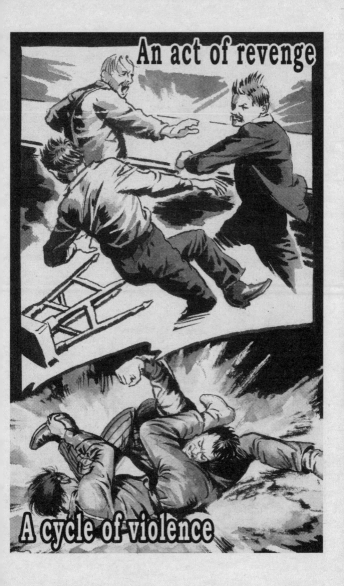

In Louis L'Amour's classic tale of loyalty and betrayal . . .

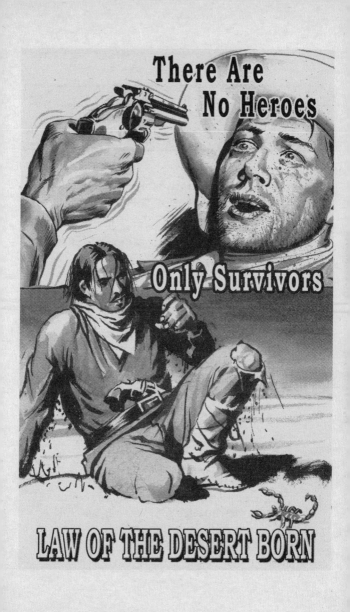